The Elephant's Claw is the first collection of short stories by W. Terence Walsh. Each story is set within an idealised post-war Britain – when the NHS was still new, when international travel was beyond the reach of most, when telephones were mostly to be found in red boxes on street corners, when tenement slums were bulldozed to make way for brutalist modernism, and people enjoyed picnics, pipe-smoking and periodicals. Just like any other era in human history, it was a time of fear, loss, and confusion – endured by most with a stoic sense of silent, pensive dread.

The Elephant's Claw

A collection of short stories
by W. Terence Walsh

First published in 2020.
This paperback edition published in 2020.

ISBN: 9798674357926
Independently published

I dedicate this collection to my family,
and to those kind souls who have
recommended good books to me over the years.

Contents

Foreword.......... 9

The Referral.......... 13
The Host.......... 29
The Mountain.......... 39
The Corner.......... 53
The Post.......... 65
The Chair.......... 75
The Hotel.......... 85
The Threshold.......... 101
The Burden.......... 109
The Vessel.......... 121
The Witness.......... 137
The Ghosts.......... 147

About the author.......... 165

Foreword

The elephant's claw sat on a small lamp table in my Great-Aunt Coral's drawing room, resting regally on a square of tasselled blue velvet, capturing the slowly tilting Sunday afternoon sunshine that poured through the bay window. On our weekly family visits, the grown-ups would engage in the incomprehensible chatter that occupied the strata above my eight-year-old head, hair neatly combed, sitting quietly nibbling a digestive biscuit (if I was lucky). Bored rigid, my attention would be magnetically drawn to the eccentric brass ball, about three inches in diameter, its upper half covered in intricate etched patterns while its southern hemisphere was composed of a cage of radial claws, curving inwards towards its pole.

Coral would invariably notice my fascinated gaze and, with the briefest of waves delivered mid-conversation, grant permission for me to carefully pick up the mesmerising object and give it a gentle shake. Magically, a resonant bell tone would fill the air, clear and true, gradually diminishing in volume but never quite receding into silence. The grown-ups would smile in my direction, as if I had performed some conjuring trick, before my mother would silently encourage me to replace the bell with eyes that were equally kind, patient and authoritative. Do *not* drop it, child.

The story went that Coral's long-deceased husband, Cedric,

had travelled a fair bit during his career as a diplomat. Coral's home, a substantial but crumbling suburban villa, was filled with exotic mementoes that included a Zulu warrior's shield, a Mauser rifle used in the Boer conflict (firing pin removed, of course), an incongruously tiny piece of Chinese calligraphy in a very large frame, and a spectacularly ornate silver teapot from Calcutta.

The elephant's claw was also a trinket from India. Attached to the animal's harness, these bells warned passers-by to get out of the way lest they be trampled underfoot. Naturally, the name caused some confusion in my juvenile mind. Elephants with claws? That simply could not be. When it was explained to me that the item took its name from its own appearance rather than any anatomical reference to the species it adorned, I was still a little confused. Why would an elephant need a bell? Elephant's were huge. They trumpeted their arrival, quite literally. They could hardly be missed walking down a street. I would imagine the pandemonium cased by any pachyderm tramping down the middle of the road outside Coral's house, flanked by neat privet hedges, with the neighbours screaming and waving their handkerchiefs in the air. The fantasy would make me smile at first, but then always filled me with a sticky melancholy.

Years later, when Coral finally passed away, she generously left me a meagre sum of money in her will and a box containing the elephant's claw and a brief handwritten note: 'I always hated this thing. Your loving aunt, C.'

Since my inheritance, the bell has followed me around from address to address. It currently acts as a paperweight that sits on top of the manuscript beside my typewriter, holding the growing pile of foolscap folio in place, which is particularly useful on those days when I decide to open the window of my study.

I often gaze upon it and consider my childhood confusion

regarding its seemingly redundant purpose. Why would one need to be alerted to the presence of something so huge and obvious as an elephant? However, the more I have thought about it, we all need to be reminded from time to time of the elephant standing in the corner of the room. The beast that waits silently, biding its time, as we fritter and waste ours, until we are ready to confront the enormity of its presence – undoubtedly at the last moment of our existence, when we simply no longer have the means or the will to go on ignoring something that is plain as day.

I hope the stories contained within this collection act like the claw bells hanging from the elephant's harness. Clear and true, resonating and vibrating in ways that warn the reader of that which is so obvious and yet so hidden. Those curious enormous things that hide in plain view from us all.

W. Terence Walsh
Summerhill, Kent
3 September 1969

The Referral

The symptoms had been present, on and off, for six weeks. Never quite debilitating enough to require leave from work or other commitments, but noticeably and semi-permanently present in the form of a nucleus of anxiety lodged somewhere between the top of the spine and the base of the skull. One dreary Monday morning, following a hostile weekend defined by an anxious seed cramping my stomach, I resolved to telephone Dr Benton's surgery from the payphone in the hall, keeping my voice low so as not to reveal any specific details to the neighbours downstairs. By Thursday I was sitting across from Benton's corpulent, affable face, rolling down my shirt sleeve and waiting with anticipation for the good doctor to make a pronouncement. Over the coming months, various remedies were prescribed, with scripts for chalky pills and milky syrups being diligently dispensed and diligently consumed in an effort to isolate and treat the roots of several suspected problems. After a quarter year of review appointments, Benton sat back in his chair, wiping his hands with a ball of cotton wool soaked in sterile solution, puffed out his cheeks and tossed the swab into a metal bin. Grabbing his fountain pen, he filled in a form recommending a specialist referral and bade me farewell with the promise that a letter would be dispatched in due course.

Life carried on as usual for a number of weeks. The familiar routine continued – commuting on the bus, days of work, lunches, dinners and evenings trying to relax, reading in bed. The symptoms were now persistent. Never quite bad enough to warrant a full day in bed, but prompting a diet of soups, early nights, and a long lie on Saturday mornings when the strain of the week's work finally abated. The usual trips to the tennis club and outings to the cinema had been indefinitely put on hold. Following the referral, diagnosis, and ultimately a successful treatment, I would make a point of planning an evening to a restaurant to celebrate. Maybe even arrange a fitting for a new suit.

I was descending the stairwell one morning when I bumped into the postman who handed over a white envelope, emblazoned with the inky blue crest of the local health service. The text on the front made it crystal clear the communication was not a circular and that important information was enclosed, but still I placed it unopened in my satchel and made my way to the bus stop in my normal fashion. Sitting on the top deck of the bus, I was acutely aware of the envelope now finally in my possession – something that could, in a very literal sense, be life changing. I felt the letter radiate its power through the brown leather of the satchel and onto my lap. I waited until I was settled at the office and, after opening all of the work correspondence waiting on my desk and attending to the most pressing duties of the morning, I carefully sliced open the envelope and allowed my eyes to bounce down the three paragraphs of neatly typed and formally polite text. Looking at my desk calendar, I calculated that the date for the referral appointment was approximately four weeks hence. My heart rate was fractionally elevated. I felt as if a journey was beginning, although I had no real idea of its nature and only an oblique notion of its destination.

The evening before the appointment, I chose to walk home from work rather than taking the bus. It was dusk and the streetlamps were only beginning to come on as I meandered through the suburbs on my route homewards. Looking through windows, I saw families laying out cutlery on dinner tables, fathers being welcomed home by eager young children, wives being kissed on cheeks, steam rising from pots on stoves. I wondered about my own future. A chance to pass on the financial fruits of my career, my knowledge and my skills to a family of dependants. Turning into my street, I saw a man standing in his living room, dressed in his hat and overcoat, holding a glass of whisky in his hand. His spectacles reflected the flickering light of a television set. His expression was one of complete blankness, his lower jaw grinding slowly.

Following a meal of tinned soup and bread, I cleaned the dishes and listened to a light music programme on the transistor radio, and then took a bath. I had been looking forward to a relaxing soak, but the water was lukewarm from the tap and became unpleasantly frigid rapidly, forcing me to stand for a while in front of the electric radiator in a towel before donning a set of clean flannel pyjamas. I returned to the kitchen to warm some milk and set out my bus timetable, a free map of the borough I had picked up earlier from an estate agency, and my hospital appointment letter. In my mind's eye, I followed the route I would take tomorrow by bus. I went to bed at 9pm, although I wasn't tired in the slightest. It was a good two hours before I finally drifted off to sleep. As I lay in bed watching the patterns of distant car headlamps on the ceiling, I went over the script I had prepared to describe my symptoms to the specialist, imparting all of the key pathological details in a succinct manner, but without coming across as needy, wheedling, long-winded, or as a know-it-all.

I was at the office for 8.50am. The timing of my appointment meant I would need to leave again at 9.30am, but I felt it would look bad if I simply took the whole morning off. In the half hour I spent at the office, I declined the offer of a cup of tea, worried this would in some way skew the results of any medical tests that might be carried out later. I looked absently at some financial ledgers for a while but my mind was elsewhere. I left the office at 9.20am.

The bus journey to the clinic was circuitous and unusual, taking me through parts of the town I had never seen before. I passed terraces of soot-filled slums, modernist factory buildings under construction, areas of woodland. I passed a gaudy petrol station, built on the site of a church bombed during the war. It took almost an hour to reach the hospital. The final part of the journey was along a straight, tree-lined road which ended in a roundabout at the hospital entrance. After alighting, the bus circled before retracing its route back to the town centre. As the din of the diesel engine receded, I realised it was noticeably quieter here than in the town and the sky seemed more expansive somehow. The silence reminded me of a childhood trip to an island off the west coast of Scotland. I was at the end of the line.

I found myself staring at a large information sign with a baffling list of acronyms and clinical departments, each accompanied by a blue arrow. I checked my letter to see which clinic I was supposed to report to (despite the fact I had reread the letter several times that morning), but the name wasn't on the sign. I set off along a path that led to the 'Main Reception' – a long, low building with a flat roof and a set of rotating glass doors. A groundsman was trimming the edges of the lawn adjacent to the path with a pair of long-handled clippers. When he looked up, one of his eyes looked directly at me while the other gazed off somewhere beyond my right shoulder. I bade him a polite good morning. He held my gaze with his good eye but failed to make any response, verbal or otherwise. As I turned my head and continued towards the entrance, I heard his clipping resume, but more slowly than before.

The main reception area was smaller than I expected, with just one nurse seated behind a perspex counter with circular conversation holes, rather like a teller in a bank. I presented my appointment letter, slipping it through the gap beneath the window, and she responded by telling me to follow the green arrows until I saw the raven. Slightly perplexed, I was about to ask for more details when her telephone rang and she picked up the receiver, pointing the direction for me to go with a gesture that was helpful but also felt like she was shooing me away. I noticed a series of coloured arrows in the linoleum at my feet and set off following the green route. I felt like a small child on a treasure hunt.

I walked through a series of antiseptic corridors past the occasional staff member and fellow out-patient, until the various colour-coded arrows began to disperse. Orange went its own way, then yellow and finally blue. A solitary green line on the floor led me into a wing of the hospital which seemed to be thinly populated and remote by comparison. Looking up, I saw a large modernist oil painting on the wall directly in front of me. It was an abstraction, but unmistakably a black raven. To one side was an open doorway leading to a waiting area – plastic chairs, a low table scattered with magazines, vertical blinds on the windows. I walked to the reception window and rang the bell on the counter and waited for a response. The window was frosted with vertical panes, not unlike the lens of a dentist's lamp or a lighthouse, and I could see a blurred figure behind the window moving. I became aware that the waiting room itself was uncomfortably warm. A low radiator that ran the length of one wall was making a churning noise. A small electric fan sat on the countertop. A handwritten note had been taped to the base: 'Do not use.'

I waited for half a minute, watching the figure move around

behind the window and considered ringing the bell again. Just then a man entered the room behind me and approached the counter. He was in his seventies, with a Persian appearance, dressed in a well-tailored grey suit, very tightly fitted, with a small white flower in his button hole, a silk cravat and a grey velvet hat. He removed the hat to reveal a head of jet black curly hair, parted to one side, not unlike Charlie Chaplin. There was a faint smell of lemons radiating from him. I noticed he wasn't wearing any socks under his highly polished black patent shoes. As he approached the counter, the glass window slid to one side immediately. The reception nurse lent forward and began a conversation with him in hushed, urgent tones. After this brief exchange, the man made a brief bow towards the nurse, turned on his heels with the grace of a dancer and took a seat.

"Yes?" said the nurse, this time addressing me. Without a word, I handed over my appointment letter. She held a pair of half-rimmed spectacles up to her eyes. The older gent made a rattling cough behind my back, followed by a spitting noise. I didn't look. "Please take a seat," said the nurse without looking up. She slid the window closed, taking my appointment letter with her.

I sat down in a chair on the opposite side of the room to the old man and picked up a periodical. I noticed that he wasn't reading and instead was looking directly up at the ceiling. I leafed through the magazine and found an article about sailing holidays. I had no intention of ever taking a sailing holiday, but the topic piqued my interest. A few paragraphs in, I became aware that the piece wasn't so much a travelogue, but a work of dramatic fiction. Two sisters had been kidnapped by pirates whilst sailing through the Mediterranean. They were being held captive in their own vessel and were planning to murder their captors in order to escape. But then the story began to go into great detail regarding the catering available on board, the quality of the linen on the beds and the wonderful sunsets that could be enjoyed from specific marinas in the Balearics. Curiously, no further mention was made of the pirates and the sisters. At the end of the piece was an italicised paragraph with a phone number to call for more information on 'chartering our luxury four-berth sloop, with highly capable African crew available for a negotiable fee.'

I noticed that the older man was no longer in the room. He must have left without a sound. I could hear footsteps approaching from behind the reception counter and decided to put my magazine down, in case I was to be called next. Out of the corner of my eye I saw a movement and turned instinctively in the direction of the doorway. Momentarily, I saw the old man's face, grinning a toothless smile, retreating smoothly through the doorway – but at a height of only a foot or so above the ground, as if he were crawling on his hands and knees. I was about to address him when the glass windows slid back with a terrible scraping noise and the nurse called out my full name twice in quick succession. I stood up with a start, looking briefly at the now empty doorway, before making my way to the counter.

"Please turn left outside the door, please follow the corridor to the end, and please take a seat in Waiting Area B. Mrs Carmichael will attend to you presently, thank you." The unsmiling nurse waited for a moment and then lifted a finger to direct me towards the door.

I made my way into the corridor, half-expecting to see the old man crawling along the floor, but there was no one. Just the lingering scent of lemons. I passed several doors marked with alpha-numerical codes. Behind one of the doors, I could hear a muffled conversation between two people, punctuated by a loud peal of laughter. Shortly, I arrived at a large letter B on the wall. There was a single plastic chair positioned beside a door. I noticed a metal plaque engraved with the words 'Mrs F. Carmichael' in utilitarian lettering.

Sitting down, I discovered that I was quite fatigued. I had expected to be anxious and even thrilled by what lay next. I had meticulously planned for this day in the hope that my malaise would finally be identified and a suitable course of treatment would be delivered. I had pinned much hope on the outcome of the next few moments. However, in reality, I felt jaded, exasperated, overheated and out of breath – my overriding urge was to lie down somewhere and restore my energy.

The door opened beside me and Mrs Carmichael ushered me in to her surgery with a simple, "Come, come." By the time I got to my feet and followed her into the office, she was already seated behind her desk, writing in a notebook rapidly with a silver ballpoint. She was left-handed, I noticed. 'Sinister', to use the Latin term. I remembered something Benton had said several times in relation to my symptoms: "I'm sure it's nothing sinister."

She was a slim woman in her fifties, with long, red hair parted in the middle. Her hair was wavy, as if it had been recently removed from plaits, but appeared to be held in position by some kind of lacquer. Her face was slightly obscured, tilted down to her notebook, but I could discern that her skin was very pale and smooth, like porcelain, with faint blue veins visible at the temples. Timidly, I sat on the chair in front of her desk with my overcoat and satchel on my lap. She appeared so engrossed in her work, it felt inappropriate to disturb her industry.

I took a moment to look around the room. On the wall behind the desk there were three framed photographs. The first showed Mrs Carmichael and what I assumed to be her husband in evening dress meeting with a dapper-looking dignitary wearing a mayoral necklace. No one was smiling. The second photograph showed a red setter on a neatly trimmed suburban lawn. The third was an aerial photograph of what looked like a small modernist university campus set in dense woodland.

"Now then." Mrs Carmichael emphatically clicked the retractable nib of her pen, placed it down neatly and steepled her fingers in front of her face. She looked directly at me with almost unnaturally grey eyes. She had just the hint of a smile upon her face. After a brief moment I opened my mouth, about to launch into my well-rehearsed catalogue and history of symptoms, but Mrs Carmichael hushed me by closing her eyes and bringing one index finger to her lips. She remained in this position for about ten seconds – which, in a situation such as this, feels like an eternity – until she relaxed and began to speak in a steady, measured voice.

"I have closely studied Dr Bendix's notes and everything is in order. I now know exactly what the problem is, and exactly how to treat you. It is imperative that you follow my instructions – *to the letter* – for the next two weeks. I am confident you will soon begin to feel much better. I will now write a prescription for you, which you will take today to the hospital dispensary, which is in the same room as the reception. Do you have any questions?"

I was slightly at a loss for words. So many months of anxiety to now be told I would feel better within a fortnight! Despite the unusual timbre of her voice and the mechanical syntax of her sentences, I felt a deep warmth towards Mrs Carmichael and instantly recognised that I had reached an important milestone in my recovery – a reward for my patience and stoicism.

"Thank you so much, Mrs Carmichael. I feel I owe you a great debt of gratitude already, even before my treatment has begun."

"Not at all, you are very welcome."

"Just one question. You mentioned Dr Benton, but I think

you called him Bendix?"

She began scribbling on a prescription pad. "Oh, I forget sometimes about his new name! You must forgive me. I studied with Felix before the war and it's hard for me to change my old ways. We used to call him Ninety-Nine you know, on account of the double IX suffixes in his name. Although that, of course, is a misnomer as the correct numeric would be XCIX." She tore the script from her pad and held it out to me. To be more accurate, she held it away from herself, even looking away from me until I took the paper from her hands.

"I will see you again in two weeks. Good day and good luck." She returned to focussing on the papers on her desk. Slightly unsure how to properly end the encounter, I half-mumbled another thank you before standing up, somewhat clumsily clutching my coat and satchel, before retreating to the door. I found, to my dismay, that the door would not budge until I forcefully pulled it towards myself, almost but not quite cracking my head in the process. I exited Mrs Carmichael's surgery feeling a curious mix of relief and confusion.

Retracing my steps along the corridor, away from the raven, I furtively looked at the script in my hand. I had a curious feeling of guilt, as if I were reading a correspondence meant for someone else which, in a sense, it was. The handwritten description of my medication was detailed as: 'CH(PSY-X10), to be taken once nightly before bed for a period of two weeks only.'

The heat of the reception area seemed to have intensified as I rang the countertop doorbell for the second time that day. Presenting my dispensary note to the nurse, she returned shortly afterwards with a paper bag containing my medication. Without saying goodbye, she closed the frosted window one last time and I made my way back along the increasingly colourful corridors until I was finally outside the building. Checking my watch, I realised it had been almost an hour since the bus had dropped me off. I took a moment to simply stand still and enjoy the tranquillity of the moment, allowing my breathing to regulate to a more relaxed pace. It was a pleasant spring morning and the cool air felt like a tonic. The sky was overcast with a thin layer of milky, diffuse cloud. The sun clearly visible as a perfect yellow disc that could be gazed upon quite comfortably with the naked eye. I felt as if something was melting in my stomach. A knot of tension was gradually dissolving. I closed my eyes for a moment and listened to a distant sparrow. The clip-clip of the gardener's tools woke me from my reverie. He was quite some distance away, working on an unruly looking shrub, staring in my direction. I began to feel a little uncomfortable and walked back to the roundabout to await the bus that would take me back into town. It was only when I was settled on the top deck that I remembered my medication. Looking inside the paper bag, I was slightly taken aback to see a small grooved vinyl disc, like any typical gramophone record, but only four inches in diameter. The circular card inlay at its centre had a typewritten label with my name and some instructions: 'Play once before bed for two weeks at 33rpm. May cause drowsiness and other alterations.' Frankly, I was prepared to try anything.

Despite a slow and relatively unproductive afternoon at the office, I arrived at home that evening feeling exhausted from the day's exertions. I had little appetite and prepared a simple meal of bread, cheese and a slice of cooked ham. On a whim, I decided to open a bottle of stout and drank it off in two or three long swallows. After tidying away the dinner dishes I retired to the living room and placed the prescription on the turntable of my record player. I sat down in my armchair, then got up again quickly to turn off the room lights. Settling back into my chair, the audio recording began to fill the room.

There was a piano, recorded in a large hall, playing a simple, slow refrain over and over – two notes in a major interval followed by two in a minor key. Happy, sad, happy, sad. There were also two voices, a man and a woman, talking softly in a language I didn't understand – possibly Polish or Russian or Romanian. As the recording continued, their voices gradually became more and more agitated until they were shouting, but this coincided with the recording level of their voices decreasing dramatically. The effect was such that I had to strain to hear them at all after a while. Then, with no warning, they would return at a much louder recording level, but talking very softly and calmly. This process would repeat every three or four minutes, with the piano playing all the time.

I noticed that, despite the fact the record had been playing for five minutes, the stylus had barely travelled a tenth of the way across the diameter of the disc. As the voices and piano continued, I became slowly aware of a third sound within the audio signal – a slowly increasing crackle, a bit like the static one hears on long-wave radio bands between stations, but with hints of real sounds. Waves on a shore, a train passing, leaves in trees. As this sound got louder the piano and voices became quieter, but the transformation was virtually imperceptible as it was taking place so slowly. My eyelids began to get heavier and heavier. The room seemed to dissolve around me into a huge, dark empty space, illuminated only by the little orange light on the front fascia of the record player. I became aware that the audio no longer seemed to be coming from the speakers of the radiogram, but rather from inside my head. Just before I nodded off into oblivion, I glanced down at the slowly spinning disc on the turntable and saw two tiny figures waltzing on top of the vinyl surface. Although indistinct in the dim orange light, I was convinced they were Mrs Carmichael and the old man in the grey suit from the hospital waiting room.

I awoke the next morning feeling fully refreshed and

well slept. All this despite the fact I had slept all night in the armchair. The record was still spinning, stuck on the 'play-out' groove, making a repetitive click every second or so. I switched the player off and became acutely aware of the silence in the room.

It being Saturday, I had a leisurely breakfast of coffee, eggs and toast, listening to a current affairs programme on the wireless. Shortly afterwards I took a bath and resolved to go out for a walk around the local park. It occurred to me that I hadn't been to the park in a very long time, most likely as my symptoms had prevented me from taking much in the way of physical exercise. I took my renewed vigour to be a good omen and tentatively began to wonder if the treatment, however bizarre, was having the desired effect.

After dinner, I found I was becoming a little irritable for no good reason. I decided to start the treatment as soon as the sun set and discovered that, once again, it produced a deep and dreamless sleep. For the second night I slumbered in my armchair, the sheets on my bed untouched.

Sunday was an uneventful day of housekeeping and another short stroll, this time to a wooded area behind my old grammar school. I had planned a circular route through the forest, but halfway round I decided to turn back when a sudden feeling of exhaustion came over me. By the time I reached home it was getting dark and I barely had the energy to climb the stairs to my door. I fell into my armchair and dozed for a while, still in my overcoat and scarf.

When I awoke it was after midnight. My symptoms had all but disappeared, but I now felt somewhat discombobulated – as if my internal clock was askew. Despite the late hour, I was wide awake. I prepared a snack and tidied some laundry before settling down with a cup of hot tea to listen to the late programme. By the time it reached 2am, I placed my treatment back on the record player and within twenty minutes I had drifted off. As I was losing consciousness, I became dimly aware that the sensation was distinct from the normal feeling of going to sleep. My head seemed to fall backwards against the armchair in slow steps, like the individual frames of a cine film, synchronised to my heartbeat. Then my head and neck appeared to fall through the very fabric of the armchair and into the space beyond. The normal rules of physics and gravity were diminished in some way, and my perception of time was altered, the pink noise inside my head decreasing slowly in pitch and becoming colossal in its scale and distance.

I awoke to the grey light of Monday morning feeling very tired. I was still dressed in yesterday's clothes so I walked down to the payphone and called the office to tell them I wouldn't be in today. As I ascended the staircase, a neighbour opened her door an inch and peered out at me with a single eye. We didn't acknowledge one another, despite the situation being rather obvious. I put myself to bed for the first time in days and dreamed of a large house filled with a party of strangers. I found myself in an altercation with a tall man, who was accusing me of being a nuisance. By raising my voice to prove my innocence I became aware of the paradox.

Over the following days, life became more and more unusual. I would either be adrift and unconscious in my armchair following an application of the treatment, or I would be asleep in my bed invariably returning to the arguments of the country party. In between these two states I would wander from room to room, attempting to carry out simple household duties or prepare a meal. Ultimately, I found myself getting nowhere. When I attempted to wash the dishes I spent an age looking for the missing dish-mop in every corner of the kitchen. Opening a high cupboard, I knocked over a full box of soap flakes onto the floor. This led me to focus on trying to find a dustpan which, in turn, led to me bumping my head on the underside of the still-open cupboard door. I left the mess and returned to my armchair to rest. Before too long, the kitchen looked like a bomb site and the other rooms in the flat quickly followed suit.

I had trouble discerning night from day. I tried to telephone the office one morning to update them of my absence, but couldn't get an answer. It gradually dawned on me that it was 8pm rather than 8am. After several days like this, I simply decided to give up. I gave up phoning the office, trying to get dressed, trying to tidy up, trying to eat and even trying to make it to bed to sleep. The armchair became my home. Although I was aware of all that was wrong with this turn of events, I would not admit it. Vitally, my symptoms had disappeared completely and I took great comfort in this.

At some point during the night, I switched on the turntable to perform yet another treatment. I settled back into the armchair and waited for the piano, the voices, the waves on the static shore. As usual, my perception began to take on its fragmented, frame-by-frame character and my skull slowly drifted back into the void behind the headrest of the chair. This time something was different. I was aware, for the first time, of the click of the play-out groove playing inside my head. Although to say 'inside my head' was inaccurate – my sensation of having a body was gone. I was simply an entity floating in nothingness. Sight had gone, along with touch, taste and smell. The click was still present although becoming slower and slower, quieter and quieter, the interval between each dusty pop becoming greater and greater.

A thought occurred to me. Put another way, I *became* the thought. The clicks on the record appeared to be slowing down but, in reality, my rate of being able to perceive time was exponentially increasing. I thought of a clock face and considered the possibility of measuring a tenth of a second by dividing the standard markings into smaller subdivisions. And then repeating the process to measure hundredths, thousandths, even millionths of a second. If the process continued, it was possible to imagine a way in which the perception of time is so minute, so infinite, that it dropped into an endless chasm that, for all intents and purposes, travelled in a direction that was no longer parallel to time, but was perpendicular. In effect, this perception would be outside of time. Existing in a nameless dimension that would be impossible to describe.

I felt very calm, aware there was truly no sensation I could now be aware of in the world I had left behind. Time had ceased to exist. As I finally became something else, I tried to imagine the smell of lemons, but it was pointless.

The Host

I arrived at Astoria Gardens shortly before ten o'clock. In the early autumn sunshine, the street was magnificent, albeit in a humble, suburban way. Neatly symmetrical rows of white-walled, red-roofed 1920's bungalows edged the sides of the tarmac, each with its own neatly-kept garden of manicured privet, flowering borders and trees that would bring forth oriental blossoms in spring.

Thinking back to my first-year studies, I recalled that suburban streets were cyclical in nature. Young couples would take up residence shortly after construction, families would be reared and eventually offspring would fly the nest. Parents would become grandparents and eventually give up the ghost, with the keys to the street being passed on to the next generation of young couples. Thus, residents tended to have an average age. I put Astoria Gardens in the upper 60's. People for whom the vivid colours of youth were now the desaturated, muted tones of autumn. Cake, cats and comfort. No regrets. Just waiting.

I thought of my own dear parents and the way they doted on their only child, wonderfully comforting and stifling at the same time. They had poured all their energies and resources into me and I often felt as if they expected some return on their investment that I could never quite repay. They would insist upon hearing all about my first proper academic interview later tonight, Mother gripping the phone while relaying all the vital details back to Papa like a war reporter.

At first glance, number 48 was typical of the properties in the street. A concrete path bisecting a small lawn, leading to a front door floating above two stone steps. Two bay windows like wise old eyes, with small slate rooflets for brows. The garden was neat, but not as colourful as its neighbours. One got the impression that the occupant wasn't concerned with impressing others. There was an element of quiet confidence in the air. Well-tended paintwork around the eaves and window-frames. No house name, no gnomes in the garden. The front door was a slight exception – a modernist spruce panel in the European style with a circular window. The metallic numerals 'four' and 'eight' inlaid expertly into the wood.

I rang the doorbell and waited – a youthful twenty-year-old, dressed in her conservative, tweedy suit, fixing a smile that was probably trying a little bit too hard to please. The brown leather briefcase (a gift from Mother) implied a sense of professionalism. Perhaps it was a little too new though? Anyone with a keen eye might realise straight away that I was new to this. They might judge me to be, in the mildest sense of the word, an imposter. A lace curtain twitched microscopically and I heard some movement on the other side of the door. Footsteps approaching on carpet and floorboards. I was aware of a dripping noise coming from the guttering above, measuring out the seconds before the door opened. No turning back now.

The door opened and Miss Hattersley's face appeared, eyebrows raised and smiling broadly.

"My dear! So good to meet you. Please come in, come in. Did you find me okay? It can be a little tricky for some people to navigate the way from the station. It's such a stupid question to ask really, because here you are! Come in, come in!"

Miss Hattersley was in her late sixties I guessed, but very spry and full of beans. She was slim and athletic looking – a tennis-player perhaps. Her hair was grey with white streaks, cut into a fashionable bob with a side parting. As she ushered me into her home, she gracefully pushed her hair away from her face with a flick of her finger. It was a curiously glamorous gesture. Her clothes were simple but well cut – probably tailored by a shop in the city with a century-long heritage and a double-barrelled name. Slacks, a sweater, a silk scarf, some simple accessories. Everything effortlessly thrown together, but somehow perfect. Mother would consider this woman 'showy', but would be secretly envious. I felt like a terrible frump all of a sudden, despite being four decades her junior. I gripped my briefcase nervously as I crossed the threshold and introduced myself.

"Thank you so much for agreeing to be one of our interviewees. When the university passed on your details, it was like finding a… hidden treasure! Finding a woman who has travelled as widely as you during the inter-war years is really quite rare."

Miss Hattersley was looking at me, smiling beatifically, as I rambled on nervously. She wasn't looking, so much as regarding me. Studying me. When I finished talking, there was a pregnant pause when it became quite apparent she was staring into my face with some fascination. I wasn't even sure if she had been listening to me. She broke the spell with a single word, like a balloon bursting with a pop.

"Tea?" Her eyebrows shot up an inch. I nodded meekly and followed her into the drawing room, where she invited me to take a seat on the settee before retreating to the kitchen. Now and then she would call through to me, asking about milk and sugar and discussing the weather and my train journey from the city. The walls of the drawing room were filled with old photographs, Arabic geometric wood carvings, South American fabrics, rustic Scandinavian pottery and goodness knows what other curios garnered from every corner of the globe. There was a large cinema poster, signed by the director: 'To Jude, with love, EP.' There was even a stuffed Arctic fox in one corner of the room, peeking out from behind a footstool. A stunning oil painting was hung above the fireplace – a cubist portrait of a young woman executed in a fantastical palette of pinks and greens. Despite the curious tilt of the neck and the other-worldly composition of the features, the face was quite beautiful. The girl appeared to have blue-black hair in a French bob but, to be frank, this may simply have been part of the artist's interpretation of the background shadows. With a tinkling sound, Miss Hattersley returned from the kitchen carrying a tray filled with chinaware.

"It's rooibos, imported from Rhodesia. A bit of an acquired taste, but very good for the metabolism."

As she poured the tea I noticed there wasn't an option to add milk and sugar, despite her enquiries. She had pronounced 'Rhodesia' with an Afrikaans accent, emphasising the sibilance of the 's' sound rather than the usual English 'z', and making the first syllable 'rod' rather than 'road'. I sipped the woody tea. It was unusual, but not entirely unpleasant. Maybe I could get used to it, given a bit of time.

"So. Where would you like to begin? The university said you're gathering research for a book about women who have travelled around a bit?"

"Yes, I'm assisting my professor specifically with a chapter that covers the period from 1918 to 1939, and we're particularly interested in…"

"Look, is it alright if we simply chat for a bit, dear? I have to admit that I'm a little nervous about these things and it would be good to… gradually warm up a bit."

I felt a wave of embarrassment. As if I had exposed a weakness. A more experienced researcher wouldn't have made such a fundamental mistake. That said, I found the idea of Miss Hattersley being nervous about anything to be slightly far-fetched. I felt an ulterior motive in the air. With a bashful smile, I set my pen and notepad down on the coffee table, crossed my legs and clasped my hands around my knee.

"That would be lovely," I said.

"So, you must be a post-graduate then? Tell me all about the life of a student these days."

Miss Hattersley then embarked upon a gentle interrogation of my life. She was completely uninterested in my studies, but instead wanted to know all kinds of seemingly mundane details about my everyday life. Where did young people shop for clothes? What kind of dietary regime did I follow? Did I exercise regularly? Was it acceptable for a woman to smoke on campus, or go to a bar by herself these days? After a while, I felt as if I was the one being interviewed. In fact, it felt like less of an interview and more of a medical consultation. I had that feeling of her scrutinising me again. Listening to what I was saying, but not focussing on my eyes. Instead, looking at my cheeks, my hair, my shoulders, and occasionally glancing down at my legs.

When I began to talk about my parents, she seemed to lose interest. With a sigh, she ended her questioning and relaxed back into her armchair.

"I think you're fabulous, simply fabulous!" she said, leaning forward to pat my hand. I blushed fiercely and mumbled a thank you, not quite sure what to make of things. I felt a little lost at sea, as if I no longer had control of the situation if, indeed, I had ever had it.

"You need to learn to accept compliments gracefully. In my experience, people don't really pay compliments unless they are genuine. When they make a compliment, it's the beginning of a contract. They expect an acknowledgement which, in turn, makes them feel good. So everyone wins."

I wasn't quite sure what else to say, so I lifted my teacup once again to my lips. My taste buds were becoming accustomed to the smoky flavour.

"When you get to my age, you realise that you have to make the most of life. Every. Single. Moment. It flashes by much faster that you would ever imagine. One moment you're a bright young thing with supple limbs and strong muscles and lustrous hair. And the next, you're here in Astoria Gardens with only the wireless for company and a clock ticking on the mantelpiece." She paused for a moment so we could hear the gentle tick-tock.

"Life is a gift bestowed upon us at birth. It's the only gift we are given, in fact. The only thing we truly possess. The only currency we can trade with. And, like any currency, it can be squandered away wastefully. In fact, most people hardly glimpse their potential and are far too easily persuaded to take the road most travelled. Settle down and settle for less. There is a universe of opportunity out there, just waiting to be snatched up by those who have the courage to take a risk or two."

She seemed to come to a natural conclusion in her monologue. A full stop hung in the air for a moment, or perhaps a comma. "So shall we take a little journey through the misadventures of my little life, dear? I'm sure you're itching to get through that list of questions in your notepad."

I was keen to get started, but I felt it would somehow be rude to segue straight from this woman's extraordinary philosophies on the universe into my dryly academic interview.

"That would be lovely, Miss Hattersley. Would it be possible for me to powder my nose before we get started?" I would normally feel embarrassed about asking a question like this, but I felt we had bonded somewhat over the last twenty minutes. Two gals facing the world together.

"Oh course, my dear. It's the door at the end of the hall. I'll pop the kettle on again and get us some ginger biscuits." She mentioned the biscuits with a wink in her voice.

I locked the door to the small bathroom and stood holding the edge of the basin for a moment, looking into the mirror. Sunlight was streaming in through the mottled glass, making the room glow a rich creamy vanilla. A small bar of Pears soap sat neatly in a tray. On the wall behind me I noticed an artefact from some far-flung part of the globe. A piece of tribal art perhaps, carved from a single piece of wood – a crude human figure with huge, staring skull-like eyes and a circular hole in the centre of its chest, where the heart should be. A cloud obscured the sun for the briefest of moments and I felt a curious sensation like falling within myself, a kind of telescopic shrinking backwards into the space behind my eyes. It wasn't an entirely unpleasant sensation. And then, just as suddenly as it arrived, the feeling was gone.

I washed my hands carefully, taking time to build up a lather and enjoying the sensation of meshing the fingers of each hand together. Slender, shapely and soft. Rinsing with warm water, I considered the skin tone on the back of each hand. Pale and even and not a liver spot in sight. Looking up I evaluated my face in the mirror, turning from left to right to assess my cheekbones and profile. I released my hair from its clasp and tousled it a little, enjoying the way the sunlight caught the redness in the chestnut hue. I needed a haircut though. Something more practical and more stylish. Something more independent. Something that would make a statement. Something glamorous that said, "I am, again, a force to be reckoned with." And the clothes? Well, the less said about these drab rags the better. It was understandable, given my current age and outlook. But, if I was to make something of myself in this world, I would need colour and style on my side. A flutter of electricity caused my heart to skip and, for a change, I didn't need to worry unduly. Life really was a currency and I was wealthy once again.

I returned to the quiet sitting room and looked through the window into the small garden, simply allowing myself to exist for a while. The easy rhythm of my breathing falling into sync with the ticking of the mantle clock. My mind was completely clear and still, like a mill pond, until the familiar shudder of the kitchen plumbing brought me back to reality.

There, slightly slumped in her armchair, sat the late Jude Hattersley. I looked at her corpse and assessed the body I had occupied for so many decades. She seemed much smaller from the outside. I hoped things hadn't been too awful for the girl, poor thing.

I went to the writing desk in the corner of the room and removed an envelope filled with crisp banknotes from a locked drawer. The money would be enough to get me to Switzerland for a month or two, become accustomed to my new self, maybe enjoy some skiing. The envelope also contained the details of several different bank accounts and safety deposit boxes that would keep me going for decades to come.

I grabbed one of Jude's coats and a scarf from a hook in the hallway. I spun around in front of the mirror and struck a red carpet pose, smiling over one shoulder. Funny to think that this was probably the most flamboyant gesture this particular body had ever made.

I grabbed the house keys with a flourish and stood perfectly still for a moment with my eyes closed. The house was silent, empty, at peace. The dishes in the kitchen cupboards were clean and stacked neatly. The bed was made with fresh linen. The daily milk order had been cancelled. The old Miss Hattersley had passed away and would probably be found in a week or so. But Jude Hattersley was very much alive and well and enjoying her prime.

I took a deep breath and left the house, enjoying the satisfying click of the latch as the door closed – perhaps for the last time.

Striding left into Astoria Gardens, I turned my coat collar up and revelled in the clarity of my youthful vision – the technicolour display of the trees that lined the pavement. A visit to the bank, a trip to the travel agency, a long, leisurely Italian lunch and finally an afternoon of wardrobe shopping in the boutiques of the West End. Oh, what it was to be young, independent and solvent!

There would be a lot to deal with, but these things always seemed to work out. New identity documents could always be acquired. Finances and property could be transferred. The poor girl's family would be devastated when she failed to return home, of course, but these things couldn't be helped. Even in the unlikely event of meeting them, I would carry myself differently, speak differently, dress differently and have a completely different personal history – not to mention a different name. Sadly, even the authorities would eventually lose interest in this particular case of the girl who simply went missing one day visiting an elderly lady. No leads, no motive, nowhere to point a finger.

Yes, it always worked out. With enough time and money on one's side, it always worked out.

The Mountain

"Are you sure you know what you're doing, Miss?" Lachlan's half-joke seemed to hang in the air as his Land Rover bumped its way back down the mountain track, leaving Pippa and me in the glorious isolation of the glen. As Pippa busied herself with her map and compass, adjusting the straps of her trusty canvas rucksack, I wondered if Lachlan had addressed his question to me or to Pippa? To all intents and purposes, this was a joint venture to be undertaken on an equal footing by the pair of us. Two fresh-faced young women on holiday in the Highlands, embarking on a day of mountain adventure. One demure, smiling, a little shy. The other confident with ruddy cheeks and a jaunty, robust demeanour. It was obvious that Pippa was leading the way. But perhaps Lachlan had spotted something in her that I hadn't. Something hidden behind the mask of swaggering bravado, and stories of previous expeditions. As the Land Rover's engine noise diminished to silence, I realised with a shiver of excitement that we were utterly alone. In my twenty years of life, I couldn't remember ever feeling this remote from the world.

"Come along then Becca. This hill won't climb itself you know," beamed Pippa, in her element. She set off up the track into the glen at a brisk pace, with me tagging along behind.

It had been Pippa's idea to come on holiday to Scotland. We worked together at the same school and, with the Easter break coming up, we'd agreed to take the train north and stay for a few days in a country hotel, with the main objective being to reach the summit of a Munro. In reality, Pippa had arranged our entire itinerary and I had simply paid my share and turned up at the train station on time, with my embarrassingly new hiking boots, rucksack and anorak (purchased from a store in town that Pippa had more or less frogmarched me into, having an earnest conversation with the shop assistant about the equipment I required as if I were a small child who couldn't be trusted to make the right decisions by myself). Her behaviour didn't irritate me. Pippa was the pepper to my salt and her personalty dictated that she needed someone to follow along in her wake. In return, I got to enjoy the holiday with a greater sense of freedom – having surrendered any sense of control to my companion. While Pippa looked at the map, I could look at the scenery.

It was a sunny day for March. The air was considerably cooler here than at home, but it felt cleaner. Lachlan had said the forecast on the wireless that morning had been favourable, but warned us to be careful, as conditions could deteriorate unexpectedly and rapidly on any mountain. Pippa had nodded her head in solemn agreement, following up with an anecdote about a blizzard she had experienced in the Pennines. I wasn't sure if she was trying to impress Lachlan, reassure me, or convince herself.

It would take six hours to reach the summit and return to the road where Lachlan had dropped us off. We were to call him from a remote telephone box located next to a derelict croft and he would pick us up and return us to the inn, where a hot bath, hot meal and hot whisky would provide the perfect reward for our exertions. In his fifties, he was an attractive man with a weatherbeaten face and kind eyes hidden under bushy brows. Although she hadn't mentioned it, I knew Pippa would be harbouring romantic notions of sharing a life with the man in some remote cottage, hanging out sheets on a line while two lively children played nearby with a dog. For all her blustery independence, she was desperate to find a suitable man and settle down. I, on the other hand, was in no rush. I wanted to live a little first. Scotland would be a good start, but my bookshelf at home had travel guides for France, Spain, Italy, Canada, Sweden. I wanted to see these places on my own terms, so marriage and children would have to wait – for a while at least.

As we progressed along the valley floor, Pippa – unsurprisingly – set a healthy pace, arms swinging at her sides, occasionally pointing out some interesting geological detail or local plant. At one point, a buzzard circled overhead. When I pointed towards the sky, Pippa briefly acknowledged my find but I could tell she was put out that I'd noticed the creature before she had. These minor victories always helped me to establish a sense of equilibrium in our relationship, reminding both of us that I was more than simply a passive spectator.

Pippa had planned a circular route, taking us along the glen for a few miles, then curving back on ourselves to ascend to the mountain summit, before descending a steep track that would finally reconnect to our starting point. After a couple of hours' steady trudging on the flat, the track started to ascend at an increasing gradient, taking us up onto the first shoulders of the mountain. We were both out of breath and a little red in the face by the time we decided to break for lunch, sitting on the soft tuffets of heather beside the track. The view back down the valley was breathtaking, cloud shadows playfully chasing each other across the far slopes. Looking up towards our destination, the summit was shrouded in mist that would fleetingly reveal glimpses of a heavy, rocky landscape, patches of snow, and pockets of blue-grey sky beyond. We ate our sandwiches in silence, passing the Thermos to each other wordlessly. Aside from the gentle noise of the wind in the heather, it was uncannily still in the lee of the mountain. It felt good to be here. Pippa and I smiled at one another. A little telepathic confirmation of shared contentment. After a few moments, she broke the spell by brushing her hands together, scattering crumbs into the wind and standing up with an emphatic, "Right-ho." A minute later we were back on the track, the half empty Thermos clanking rhythmically in time to Pippa's footsteps.

The going was tough for a while as the track continued to rise. But, before long, we finally reached a wide saddle that offered a more forgiving gradient. I suggested taking a breather, but Pippa was on a mission to reach a specific point on the map before we took another break. We hiked on for a while up the empty mountainside, the track disappearing into the clouds in front of us, with only a few boulders here and there to break up the landscape. The saddle stretched out to the left and right of us, like an elevated moor, not offering much in the way of a view. The wind picked up into a gusty breeze, and I pulled the toggles of my anorak hood a little tighter. Pippa was about twenty yards ahead of me. When she turned to say something, it was impossible to make out her words over the noise of the wind. A few moments later, I started to feel the sting of sleet on my cheeks as the hail pelted the canvas of my hood. The clouds seemed to have closed in very rapidly all around us, but the misty glare of the sun was still just perceptible overhead. Hopefully this would just be a quick shower. Pippa was calling something to me and pointing to some boulders in the distance. I assumed she was suggesting we could take shelter until the shower passed. I saw her break into a slow jog and then, strangely, she seemed to tilt sharply to the right as one of her legs disappeared into the ground. And then she was very still, simply looking down at the ground.

By the time I caught up with her, I knew something was wrong. Her face was blanched white and her usual expression of gutsy hockey-field exuberance had been replaced with an open, childlike look of confusion. Her right leg had gone into a rabbit hole, up to the knee, and she was propping herself up with her right hand, struggling to lift herself upwards. I let her put her arm around me as I grabbed her waist, and hoisted her into a standing position using all my might. As her leg came out of the ground, she gingerly placed her foot on the heather, winced, groaned, and then was sick all down the front of her anorak. Looking down at her hiking boot, it was clear that something was amiss. No blood, but the angle of her foot was twisted at the ankle through a greater number of degrees than should normally be possible.

"Don't worry, old girl. Let's get you over to these boulders for a bit of shelter." I tried to sound as reassuring as possible, as if I was going to put the kettle on to make us a nice cup of tea. The sleet had eased off a little, thank goodness, as I helped Pippa to hop across the uneven ground to the boulders. When she finally managed to find a spot with some protection from the wind, she closed her eyes and grimaced, as if all the pain had finally arrived at once.

"Are you sure you know what you're doing, Miss?" Lachlan's words popped into my mind, unhelpfully.

We spent the next hour making Pippa as comfortable as possible and discussing our options. With a broken ankle, there was no way we could get her off the mountain without help. So, it was decided that I would go on my own to get help, leaving Pippa with enough food, water and warm clothing to manage for a few hours until the cavalry arrived. For myself, there was the option of backtracking down the mountain and back into the valley, which would take about five hours, the last three of which would be in darkness. Or, I could continue towards the summit and take the quicker, steeper route down to the road. Pippa assured me this would only take two hours and I would be back at the telephone box by sunset. I could tell this was wishful thinking – she was afraid to be on her own any longer than she needed to be. Neither of us openly acknowledged the fact that an extra three or four hours' wait could have dire consequences in terms of, God forbid, hypothermia. Some atavistic knowledge seemed to be telling me that any delay would be unwise.

I gave Pippa an extra jumper from my rucksack, the logic being that I would be walking at pace and therefore keeping my body temperature up. Likewise, Pippa kept the Thermos and what was left of the sandwiches, cheese and cold cuts. She offered me the map and compass but I simply giggled, saying that they would just weigh me down. Geography was not my strong point. Besides, all I needed to do was follow the track to the summit and down again. The only item from our itinerary that caused a little confusion was the small battery-powered torch. Pippa wanted me to have it so that I could see my way in the dark. I wanted Pippa to keep it so we could find her later on. I won the argument. To be honest, I didn't want to imagine a scenario where I would be wandering around in the dark on my own. I shivered involuntarily.

"Right then, all set? I'll be back in a jiffy with a bottle of whisky and Lachlan to carry you down the mountain." We were both smiling, but there was fear behind the words. I realised I'd never been in a situation like this before. I was very fortunate that the Blitz hadn't really played a part in my childhood, being a country lass. I hugged Pippa tightly for a long time. When I finally got up to leave, she was wiping a tear from her eye. With an embarrassed smile, she batted me away. "For goodness sake, just get going you dolt! And watch out for those blasted rabbit holes."

Grabbing the straps of my rucksack with determination, I set off quickly towards the summit path, only looking over my shoulder twice to check on Pippa's pitiful figure hunched against her boulder. I knew my decisions over the next few hours needed to be sound. Every step I took could be life-changing. But the enormity of my situation was too large to comprehend. All I could do was keep my head down and focus on getting back to the telephone box as quickly as possible. With a sense of glacial panic I checked my pockets for coins and found a handful of change I could use to make the call. I wondered if emergency calls would be free of charge anyway. Should I call the inn, or the police? Oh God, what a pickle.

I followed the track for an hour or so as it gradually climbed into the clouds. There had been one or two sleet showers, but nothing too dramatic and, in general, I was pleased with my progress. Walking through the mist, I sensed that the sun was descending somewhere over to my right, and the quality of the diffuse light was changing from afternoon to evening. Any breaks in the mist directly overhead revealed much higher clouds, illuminated in a creamy glow from the oblique sunlight.

I slowly became aware of a change in the conditions. The wind was dropping considerably, and the mist around me seemed to be changing in texture, becoming sparser and lighter. The track also began to ascend quite steeply into the cloud, which was now the colour of vanilla ice cream. And then, quite suddenly, I emerged above the clouds into the glare of the setting sun.

It was such a shock, I had to stop for a minute to take in what I was seeing. Directly in front of me, the mountain peak soared up into the sky, massive, imposing, godlike. Behind me, I was able to look down onto a sea of clouds that stretched to the horizon. It was utterly beautiful, utterly alien. I had moved into a different world, like a balloonist. Occupying a different stratum of life. Separated from Pippa, from civilisation, from all of history. In a sense, I had been reborn. The slate of my life had been wiped clean. I felt I could be whoever I wanted to be. I looked back towards the summit with a renewed sense of vigour and returned to the climb.

The next thirty minutes were hard going. A series of steep inclines that led to a series of false summits, the true peak curiously and dishearteningly seeming further away at each reveal. Eventually, I arrived at the final section – a picturesque hillock rising out of an elevated shoulder with a white concrete triangulation pillar at the top. The track zig-zagged ever upwards until, unexpectedly, I found myself on the summit. The breeze was gusty but bearable so I decided to take a moment to gather my thoughts and catch my breath. I turned through a full circle, taking in the view. A spectacular sea of flat cloud, bathed in the peach light of the setting sun. I thought of the mashed parsnip we had been served at dinner the night before. The reddening orb of the sun was just an inch above the clouds while, on the opposite horizon, a huge yellow full moon had risen. It was a surreal vista. Like some kind of heavenly clock face with me at the centre. The moment would have been entirely different if Pippa and I had reached the summit together – grounded in the earthly aspect of physical achievement and companionship. Being here alone, surrounded by the infinite cosmos, I felt a spiritual charge that I had never felt in any church. Looking directly upwards the sky was an inky royal blue at its zenith. Night was coming. I set off down the track that would return me to the safety and the reality of human things.

Leaving the complexities of the rocky summit behind, the track quickly settled into a steady descent. As Pippa was fond of telling me, descending was often harder on the legs than ascending and I found the exertions of the day, and the adrenaline in my metabolism, were starting to take their toll. There was an emptiness in my belly and, when I stopped to rest, I felt a little light-headed. As the light began to fade, I cursed my decision to leave the torch with Pippa. The detail and colour of the twilight landscape were starting to disappear, replaced with monochrome folds and shadows, starkly lit by the icy light of the rising moon.

The cloud plateau was rising up to meet my progress, filling me with an unexpected anxiety. At least here, in the clear, the moon and stars could provide a sense of direction and enough ambient light to judge the nearby topography. I knew that returning into the clouds would be deeply unsettling. I imagined a dark grey void filled with uncertainty. Unseen cliffs. Thorny brambles. Nocturnal animals with sharp teeth.

About five minutes away from the cloud line I froze in my tracks. The moonlight behind me was casting a long shadow onto the slowly shifting water vapour beneath me. My outline was clearly visible, a lonely human figure surrounded by a spectral halo of incandescent colours. A ghostly apparition facing towards me, blocking my way. The hairs on the back of my neck rose and I felt my heartbeat quicken. I was not a superstitious person. But the idea of advancing towards this 'shadow ghost' filled my heart with a leaden blackness. I was petrified, turned to stone.

With a great effort, I resumed my descent slowly. The ghost figure began to move, seemingly moving closer as I neared the clouds, mirroring my movements mockingly. I halted my progress once again, staring directly at the spectre for fear that it would lunge if I should blink. I slowly raised my left arm and watched in horror as the ghostly figure twisted out of shape momentarily as the clouds shifted. A moment later, the figure reformed into the shape it had borrowed from my presence. But, from my point of view, it hadn't raised its arm.

This was getting silly. Thinking of Pippa, I steeled myself to move forward. This was simply an optical illusion caused by the unique positioning of some water vapour, a human being, and some celestial bodies. Unusual, novel, remarkable, but not anything to be afraid of. I set off again and within twenty yards I was, literally, face to face with my shadow. I closed my eyes for a moment as I descended into the clouds like a swimmer easing themselves into a pool.

When I opened my eyes, everything was shrouded in murky darkness. I could just about see the track ahead of me for about ten yards. The sound of my footsteps had changed, somehow blanketed by the mist. In contrast to the timeless infinity at the top of the mountain, I was now existing in the smallest of bubbles. A horrid, compressed existence in which time itself seemed to have lost some of its dimensionality. Looking over my shoulder, I could only just see the faint moonlight illuminating a circular patch of mist. Naturally, my mind filled in the gaps and placed the ghostly figure faintly within the spotlight. I turned quickly and carried on my way, reminding myself not to look back again. The Bible story of Lot's wife came to mind.

As I carried on into the mist, gradually the light faded and the visibility deteriorated. Before too long, I was walking like a blind person, arms stretched out in front of me, feeling at my feet to check for rocks. A sense of hopelessness descended over me and I sat down with my knees pulled up closely to my chest. Tears began to well up in my eyes. I rubbed them away with the heel of my hand and let out a huge sigh. I felt like a lost child.

"It'll be okay," whispered a faint voice.

Every muscle in my body seemed to contract as my eyes widened into saucers. With my jaw set, I looked around searchingly into the mist, but there was nothing and no one to be seen.

"It'll be okay, keep going."

This time, pure fear was replaced with a much more intricate spectrum of emotions, some of which were entirely new to me. A wave of new colours seemed to be breaking over me – the rich glow of love, the sharp tenderness of responsibility, the aching flame of worry, all mixed together into something eternal and unspoken. Nothing could stop the tears from coming now, and the high wail that rose within me from some ancient place. It wasn't until many years later that I fully understood what I was feeling at that moment – it was my first fleeting glimpse into the intensity of motherhood.

Time passed for an unknown period. I was lost somewhere within myself, surrendering to the primal forces at work. Swimming back up to the surface of my consciousness, I saw the faintest of lights in the distance. A yellow glimmer that rose and fell in intensity and danced playfully. A wisp.

As I rose up slowly into the reality of my situation, I began to understand what I was looking at. It was a torch, coming up the mountain track towards me. There were footsteps too. And a voice. A man's voice with an accent.

"Are you okay, Miss? I had a feeling something might be wrong, so I… where is the other young lady?"

My tiny world was filled with torchlight. Millennia of ingenuity pouring outwards, banishing darkness and restoring order in an instant. Time had returned to the present.

"I'm fine Lachlan, just fine. Thank you. We need to get to Miss Featherstone quickly though. She's had a fall."

*

I'm sitting in a deck chair on the lawn. It's a scorching hot June day, mid-afternoon. Walking home from school, I promised

Phoebe an ice-cream soda and now she's playing with a watercolour set on the grass while I try to read a novel. I'm finding it hard to concentrate in this heat. I close my eyes for a moment and enjoy that uniquely luxurious feeling of the sun beating down on my face. A rarity to be savoured and stored away for the winter months. My eyes see only the diffuse orange of my eyelids, curious symmetrical patterns dancing across my field of view. I open one eye the tiniest fraction. The crystal blue of the sky coalesces with rotating starbursts of liquid sunlight, filtered gently through my lashes. A bee buzzes past and I hear the tinkle of Phoebe's paintbrush in her water jar. She's humming a little tune to herself, an old folk song she learned at school. The teacher allowed the class to sit outside today to take their lessons under a tree.

I think about my little life. My part-time job helping at the school. My marriage. My wedding day. My amazing little six-year-old. Our plans to get a puppy this summer. My travels as a singleton to Menton, Paris, Rome, Biarritz, Milan. My barmy mother. My dear old dad. My happiness.

Allowing my mind to drift, I think about Pippa. She met an engineer and moved to Ireland. We still keep in touch. Birthday cards and Christmas cards. Promises to visit that come to nothing. I imagine her in her cottage, her two lively kids running between white sheets on the line, husband smoking a pipe. Huge white clouds in a deep blue coastal sky.

'The day we climbed the mountain' surfaces regularly as an anecdote that needs to be told. Once or twice a year, the subject of hill-walking will crop up in conversation with colleagues, pupils, parents waiting at the school gates, people at dinner parties. I find myself telling the story automatically – like a script. I'm remembering the previous tellings of the story rather than the event itself. The beginning of the quest, two plucky girls being thrown out of their comfort zone. The moment of disaster. The happy ending with Lachlan and his teenage son arriving just in the knick of time to save the day. Like any three act play. An ancient, cautionary tale that could, in its telling, prevent some future unfortunate from putting themselves in harm's way. Or, perhaps, encourage the listener to boldly seek out their own story of misfortune and rescue.

It's interesting that I never remark on the spiritual dimension of the story. Being the only soul above the clouds with just the moon, the stars and the cathedral peak for company. Being acutely aware of another presence existing within the clouds. My visual and auditory hallucinations, as I like to internally refer to them. The spectre and the voice. The fact is, I don't like to talk about these things because it would make them all the more real and, to be honest, I'm fearful of my memories.

I open my eyes and stretch my arms before getting up to take the empty soda glasses back into the house. As I lift Phoebe's glass, I take a look at what she has painted.

"It's beautiful, darling," I say. "Tell me all about it."

"Well that's you, Mummy. And that's me. And you're in a place that's lost. But I'm able to make you feel better because of a dream."

It's not the first time Phoebe has painted a scene like this, but the novelty never wears off. She always says it comes from inside herself and has always been there. Like a dream, but not a dream. I should be shocked or unsettled. But I'm comforted. I also know for a fact that she will gradually forget these things. Some things are only visible to small children. As she grows, the magic will fade. We all know that to be an inescapable truth, because each and every one of us has lost touch with our own childhood magic.

It's difficult to look back to that night on the mountain with any sense of objectivity. If Lachlan and his son hadn't arrived, would I have simply given up, walking in circles in the mist until I passed out from exhaustion? They said we were very lucky to be found, as a night on the mountain could have been fatal. The temperatures dropped below freezing. Pippa had to be treated for frostbite and, with some degree of pride, says she still has problems with numb toes in winter. And there was also the sheer drop, hidden just a few feet from the track. At first, I thought this particular detail had been conjured up by the locals to give our story some extra spice. But Pippa was able to show me the steep-sided, jagged-toothed corrie clearly marked on her map, the contour lines compressed unsettlingly close together.

I've tried to make sense of it all, but I always end up getting tangled up. As one part of the story becomes clear, another unravels. In the end, I like to think that I made some decisions on that night, but some were made for me. As a result, something guided me away from danger and made sure I was able to join the dots from that moment in time to this moment in time. Here, now, in my garden, with the sunlight glinting off my daughter's beautiful blonde hair.

When my grandmother passed away, my mother asked me, surprisingly candidly, where her mother's soul had gone. Without thinking, I said she had simply returned to the place she existed before her birth. We always consider ghosts to reside in the afterlife, but could they not exist in the beforelife too?

I thought of the chain of humanity linking me to my mother and her mother before her, backwards in an endless line until the beginning of time. Like all mothers, I'd managed to stay safe long enough to create something truly special. And something truly special had managed to keep me safe in return.

The Corner

I woke with a start, my head jolting up from my chest, not because of a sudden noise but rather because of a sudden silence. The train had come to a standstill and was resting at a halt. Pushing my spectacles back onto the bridge of my nose, I pressed my face up against the cold glass to peer out into the foggy gloom of the platform. A couple of benches, an overflowing litter bin, a waiting room, but no sign of a sign to indicate where I was. I checked my wristwatch which said 11.32, which was, give or take, the time I was supposed to arrive at my destination. Early by five minutes maybe. Surely there wouldn't be two stations so close together in these remote parts? And if there was, I could always hail a taxi and still be at my appointment on time. The train hissed. I grabbed my small valise and rushed toward the door at the end of the carriage.

Grabbing the handle on the window frame, I yanked it downwards and leaned outside to open the door. Despite my efforts, it appeared to be stuck fast. Looking along the length of the platform, I spied the conductor standing amid the fog, bringing his whistle to his mouth. I continued to struggle with the door, but to no avail. I began to feel the initial symptoms of panic rising up like a fluid within my chest.

"You there! Conductor! Can I get a little assistance?"

The man sauntered towards me, his rotund frame carried on tiny feet, waddling like a wheezy duck. His features emerged from the steam as he approached. Bald, with a round face composed of very white, gleaming skin. A large neck with a roll of fat bulging above a too-tight collar. The railway emblem on his tie decorated with the remains of what looked like soft-boiled egg.

"The door appears to be stuck."

After a brief but significant pause, the man stepped forward and opened the door swiftly and easily with one hand, bowing his head slightly as he held the door open for me. This, of course, was inevitable. The inept white-collar, middle-manager, officer-class oaf having to be rescued by the blue-collar, salt-of-the-earth corporal who had seen it all before and was sagely and serenely content with the stratum he occupied in life. Outwardly subservient, but inwardly a monarch of composure, genius of common sense, and tsar of silent contempt.

"Can you tell me if this is Denton?"

The man looked at me with the faintest of smiles. I saw myself briefly through his eyes. A tallish, relatively presentable gent of adequate means and intellect, who was wholly unworthy of my position due to the fact that I could not accomplish the simplest of activities. Namely, opening doors and locating myself in the world. The man nodded and said something in a dialect that was utterly unintelligible to my metropolitan ears. It was English, but not anything I could decipher. Before I could enquire further, he stepped onto the train, slammed the door shut, produced a brief, perfect shriek from his whistle and flung the window closed. The train gently began to move away, just in time for me to realise that I had left my overcoat on the luggage rack. I hadn't the heart to chase after it. For reasons I still don't entirely understand, I simply watched the train disappear into the mist with my twenty guinea overcoat still on board.

Gradually, the noise of the train was swallowed up by the fog until I was surrounded by a soft, flat silence. I walked through the deserted waiting room and out onto the station forecourt, where I could only find one official sign beside a couple of small hoardings advertising cocoa powder and cigarettes. Instead of providing me with a place name, it simply said 'Station' in the ubiquitous utilitarian lettering of the railway network. The forecourt bordered onto a country road, edged with long grass and a solitary concrete bus shelter, with an empty frame where a timetable would normally be displayed. There was a road sign indicating the direction to the 'town centre' and, beside it, a red telephone box. I stepped inside to look for any clues, but the small panel containing local advertising messages was giving nothing away. A hairdressing salon, a funeral director and a restaurant were all promoting their services on neatly printed white cards with the relevant numbers to call for more information, but none included town names. The restaurant was located in the 'high street', but that was hardly enlightening. I set off from the phone box in the direction of the civic centre, glad to be away from the faint smell of urine.

Twenty minutes later I found myself in that unusual predicament of feeling lost, despite the fact that I had simply followed a straight road without deviation. Twenty yards in front of me, the landscape disappeared into the fog, twenty yards behind me the world dissolved into an identical void. There was a dampness in the air, which produced tiny droplets of moisture on my suit jacket. There was no birdsong and no traffic noise whatsoever. Just the faintest whistle of the wind through the telegraph wires held aloft on poles that marched silently beside me.

Checking my watch, I was comforted by the fact that I still had thirty minutes before my business meeting. This comfort was entirely spurious, of course, given that I had no idea how far away from the town centre I was. I made use of my time by rehearsing my usual sales pitch. Probably the tenth speech of its kind I had delivered this week, in ten different towns. No doubt this had contributed to finding myself unexpectedly unconscious on the train. I hadn't heeded the recent warnings given by my doctor and the anxious pleading of my dear wife to regulate my schedule and give myself more rest. I was certainly no longer the virile executive of my youthful years. Sometimes it seemed that my workload and travelling commitments were *increasing* with the years, which I certainly hadn't expected to happen over the course of my career. But, what were my options? I had mouths to feed and bills to pay. This was the course I had taken through life and it was, frankly, too late to change tack. I stepped in a puddle, soaking one shoe and the lower cuff of a trouser leg. Buggery.

The solid shape of a building began to emerge from the mist. A dark, mossy, granite church, its spire gradually fading into the white fog before disappearing completely into the atmosphere. Looking at the structure, an unusual thought crossed my mind. For someone born and bred in western Europe, the sight of a church spire is so commonplace as to be almost invisible. Vaguely reassuring in its own way, and imbued with memories of village fêtes, harvest festivals, dusty sermons and woody scents. But, for someone arriving from a foreign land, a typical English church must look as exotic as an onion-spired mosque, or an oriental pagoda, or an Aztec temple. On this occasion, seeing the familiar spire of the church offered little comfort. I felt very much like a lost tourist in a strange land, far from home, and culturally disassociated from my surroundings.

Passing the church, I found myself on what must have been the main street, completely devoid of people, with a handful of cars and vans parked outside a scattering of shops. A restaurant (closed), a hairdressing salon (opening after lunch) and a funeral director (open, complete with open caskets, but with no sign of life inside). Eventually, I arrived at an intersection where the main street was bisected by another road to form a neat, symmetrical crossroads. A crossing of ways. A decision of sorts. Onwards, left, right, or back on my tracks. Standing at one corner, I heard a bell gently ring as a shop door opened diagonally across the intersection. The shopkeeper appeared in a brown tradesman's coat, picking up a stack of tied newspapers from the pavement. He smiled across at me, before disappearing inside the doorway with another chime of the bell. I made my way across the road, heading directly towards the doorway which was angled into the corner of the building, facing directly at the dead centre of the crossroads. The shop had two large frosted windows on either side of the entrance and an illuminated lightbox sign directly above the doorway that read 'The Corner of the World'. Glancing at my wristwatch, I calculated that I would have fifteen minutes to reach my appointment if the shopkeeper could provide adequate directions. Grabbing the well-worn brass door handle, I felt a small shimmer of excited confidence rush through me as the spring bell announced my arrival with a jaunty, vibrant clarity. All was not lost. Yet.

The interior of the shop was small, dark and somewhat confusing. At first glance, the floorplan didn't appear to match the exterior of the shop, with shelving set at unusual angles and tiny aisles that led off into dimly lit corners. The counter was half hidden behind a display rack filled with a mad variety of produce – vegetables, novels, gewgaws, string, hosiery. As I approached the counter, the shopkeeper emerged from an open doorway behind, parting the coloured nylon strips hanging from the frame like a swimmer performing the breast stroke.

He was a man in his sixties, with a tidy goatee beard and neatly parted grey hair. He was wearing a pair of horn-rimmed spectacles. One of the lenses was frosted and opaque, like a fragment of glass washed up on a beach. The single eye that addressed me with a friendly gaze was disconcertingly pale, like a sheepdog's, and brown in colour. So light as to be almost orange. There was some music playing quietly in the back room on a radiogram. Classical, but with eastern motifs. An oud hidden within the orchestration, perhaps.

"Hello, sir, and what can I help you with today." The shopkeeper's warm and pleasant smile combined the reassurance of experience with the humility of servitude.

"I'm afraid I appear to be a little lost. I have an appointment in Denton at half past, at the radio factory. I'd be tremendously grateful for some directions if you'd be so kind."

The shopkeeper's eyebrows shot up. "Denton! I'm afraid that's the next town over. About thirty minutes by foot, or ten if you take the bus. The next bus should be along in ten minutes or so."

I looked at my wristwatch yet again. Damnation. What a mess. I prided myself on never being late. I was sure to make a poor impression.

"You're welcome to telephone ahead? Let the factory people know you're running a little late?" He lifted a telephone on to the top of the counter and spun it around so that the dial was facing me. After a moment or two of thank yous and fussing for numbers, the call was made and my contact was aware that I would be with him shortly. I felt as if I had finally made some progress and that the tide of my fortunes was turning.

I realised I should purchase something before leaving the shop, to show my gratitude. A picked up a packet of peppermints and a newspaper and set them on the counter.

"Ah, more bad news. Nothing but bad news." The

shopkeeper gestured towards the headline as he took my change.

"I have a theory about bad news, you know. These wars and conflicts around the world, they all have to begin somewhere. They don't start with big decisions made by politicians and generals, no. They begin with people like us, the ordinary folk."

I made a quizzical look, not quite sure where this conversation was headed. The shopkeeper placed his palms downwards on the countertop and straightened his arms.

"Tiny little frustrations. All of those silly little annoyances that happen on a daily basis. A train running late. The loss of a hat or a coat. Being short-changed. Walking through a puddle. An argument with a work colleague or a loved one. All these little things build up over time to create an overwhelming pressure that needs to be released. Lots of little inconveniences become a much bigger evil. A resentment between people for simply existing. And, as the population grows and grows, the resentment becomes more intense. People are backed into their own little corners, trying to defend their little patches of land. And what happens when any animal is backed into a corner? It raises its hackles and bares its teeth of course. It prepares for attack."

I found that I was gawping at the man as he continued to speak. Wary, but also strangely transfixed. I was hanging on his every word.

"And so even the most despicable warlike acts of any nation or government can be traced back to a simple act of inconvenience. The lengthening queue at the bakery leads to the assassination of Archduke Ferdinand which leads to the industrial annihilation of a generation of souls in the trenches of Flanders. You see, that's where the real evil lurks. Not in the machine guns and artillery, but in the spilt milk and insensitive words said by siblings in the heat of the moment. The employer who belittles his staff. The teacher who bullies his pupils."

He paused to lift a stack of newspapers onto the counter.

"And all this so-called *journalism* is just grist to the mill. If you're already in a state of anxiety and anger, reading a few column inches of short-sighted polemic will help to stoke the fires of fear, paranoia, intolerance and suspicion. These days, bad news only arrives on your doorstep once a day. But, in the years to come, with television and what have you, the news will arrive instantaneously. Imagine that. An endless stream of bad news, beamed into every home, until even the meek will be infected, rising up to defend themselves from whatever bogeyman lurks just over the horizon, and inadvertently condemning themselves to a life of misery and depression, never being able to live in the moment because civil liberties, freedom and security are always at risk, hanging in jeopardy, always under threat."

The shopkeeper paused, looking directly at me with that liquid fiery eye. Looking through me and past me and into the distance. Into the future. The faintest suggestion of satisfaction spread across his face. And then, he blinked and returned his focus to the here and now.

"I think I can hear your bus. Yes, bang on time as usual. You can grab it just across the street and you'll be in Denton in a jiffy. I hope you have a good day, sir." He bowed theatrically.

As I stepped aboard the bus and drove away from the crossroads, I saw the shopkeeper come out onto the street to stare at the bus for a moment. Then, after checking his pocket watch, he proceeded to brush some litter off the pavement and into the road. His efforts made the small patch of land in front of his shop no tidier, and would probably cause problems for the next driver or cyclist who passed by.

*

The meeting at the radio factory went as well as could be expected. The people were friendly, but I could tell that my tardiness and slightly harried appearance wouldn't instil the kind of confidence they were looking for. Afterwards, I easily located Denton train station, which was a much more reassuring building than the halt I had alighted at earlier. With an hour to kill, I took a seat in the station tea room and lit my pipe while the waitress served a pot of tea with a scone.

As was my usual habit in these situations, I had the luxury of examining my fellow patrons at leisure, being a lone traveller. A couple of old women, gossiping and complaining about a young neighbour that was 'obviously up to no good with a stream of gentlemen callers arriving at all hours of the day and night.' A small child was teasing his sister, calling her names and pulling her hair. The closer to tears she became, the more delighted he seemed to be. Their mother was lost in a magazine article, most likely dreaming of another, better life in Hollywood that would never be fulfilled. Two men in flat caps were talking about football. Although the tone of their voices indicated a solemn agreement with much nodding of heads, they were in fact delivering entirely opposing arguments, each man lost in his own strategy that would lead the team to the cup final and beyond, not really listening to the other at all. And then there was me. Spying on all this grubby activity and peering down on the world with a sickly sense of superiority. A sense that was totally unjustified of course, what with me being a slightly washed-up travelling salesman.

I looked down at my hand and had a curious feeling of being outside of myself, like being the member of a different species. What would a whale, or an owl, or a wasp make of this weird, pink, fleshy square with its five stick-like digits. If they could understand our languages, what would they make of our endless prattling? Our insistence on 'standing together for the good of all' when, in reality, we were just as vicious and unfeeling and self-serving as leopards chasing down gazelles. I needed some fresh air.

Standing outside on the station forecourt, I noticed a church directly opposite. The sign outside said, 'St Katherine without Oldgate. All welcome.' On a whim, I made my way across the road and went inside. I was an irregular Sunday church goer with little sense of faith. But, on my travels, I often found that ten minutes spent within the silence and sanctity of a church could do wonders for the soul, promoting a feeling of wellbeing and peace. Reflection. A chance to look at one's self and see what was really there.

I sat down on one of the rear pews and took a moment to enjoy all the usual sensory cues. Beeswax polish, carpet on stone, particles of dust caught in sunlight. The feeling that this was a place for people, but somehow removed from humanity. The afternoon sunlight was visible in diagonal beams, cutting across the building at regular intervals. I noticed how the stained glass depiction of a saint had been transformed into a series of intricate parallel bars of light flowing through space. All the colour information of the saint's soul transported into beams of photons, optical data travelling so fast as to appear solid. Eternal. Illuminated. I took a series of slow, deep breaths, closing my eyes and emptying my mind.

On the way out, I bumped into the verger who was returning from some errand, carrying a cardboard box under one arm.

"It's a lovely church you have here," I said. I felt that, in some way, I needed to pay the compliment in order to settle my bill for taking whatever it was I had taken from the place.

"Yes, yes, indeed. We get quite a few visitors who come to Denton to visit the church on account of its unusual floor plan. There are only a handful of circular churches in the country, you see. It's quite a novelty."

I noticed, for the first time, that the church was indeed perfectly round, like a miniature Pantheon with a domed roof.

"Yes, there's quite a famous church on the Scottish island of Islay that's round, rather similar to St Katherine's in fact. Legend has it that it was built that way because there would be no corners for the devil to hide in."

"What a charming notion," I said as we both took a moment to admire the architecture in silence. Making his excuses, the verger shuffled off in the direction of a doorway at the rear of the church. That's if a circle could be described as having a rear.

As I walked back to the station to catch my train, I made a mental note to visit a travel agency to make enquiries about the cost of a holiday to Islay. My head began to fill with idealised imagery of a wild, remote Scottish landscape, sunny but windswept, and utterly devoid of the sounds that people make.

The Post

The alarm rang, like clockwork, every day at 7am. I usually had a cigarette in bed and then struggled to the bathroom to perform my morning ablutions. I always associated the word 'ablutions' with my father and his military 'career'. Too young for the Great War, too old for the next, he had served for a while in the Royal Engineers during the early 1920s before finding his true calling as a history master. The military terminology drummed into him over those years had formed the backbone of his vocabulary. He often referred to his headmaster as 'the CO', and the boys in his charge were, of course, his 'men'. His preferred stance while teaching was to take up position next to the chalkboard, rising up now and then on the balls of his feet to emphasise a point, holding his cane like a swagger stick tightly grasped between his arm and his side. As he took the boys through the various campaigns of Napoleon and Nelson, he adopted the role of a briefing officer rather than a schoolmaster, preparing his men for battle rather than examination. Silly old goat. I found myself pondering the fact that I was now older than he was when he died, poor sod.

Old age had caught up with me, it seemed. These days it took an age to go through the motions of washing, shaving, brushing my teeth, combing what remained of my hair and generally preparing for the day ahead. My own military training had made me a creature of habit in these regards, but I also liked to think I was immune to the programming I'd received. I could be spontaneous when I wanted to be and, these days, it wasn't uncommon for me to simply switch the alarm clock off and have an extra hour in bed. It was one of the few benefits of being a retiree widower – I could set my own schedule and bugger the consequences.

Once dressed, I typically had cup of tea, a boiled egg and a slice of toast with butter. I didn't listen to the radio in the morning as I preferred to get my news from the paper. Getting the paper was, in itself, a means to an end, providing an invaluable excuse to venture outdoors for some brisk exercise and fresh air (the only problem being that I inevitably had to interact with other members of the human race). Aside from those infrequent visits from Philippa and the grandchildren when they ventured across the Irish Sea to visit 'Gramps', my life was essentially a one-man show these days and that suited me down to the ground.

After putting away the breakfast dishes, I stood in front of the mirror, straightened my tie and put on my flat cap, coat and gloves. A vision of sartorial elegance in beige. I checked my wristwatch. Five to nine. That'll do. Most of the bloody straphangers would be off the street by now, safely locked away in their offices.

As I made my way towards the newsagency, I revelled in the fact that I didn't have to be anywhere at any specific time. Since retiring from my employment some years ago, the novelty of this sense of freedom had not abated. In fact, it seemed to have increased, especially since finding myself alone in the world after Jean's death. I filled the hours of my empty days with sparse activities and meagre entertainments. But the real colour of my life lay in the absolute freedom to do whatever the hell I wanted at any given moment. Of course, most of the time I would stick to a set routine but, sometimes, taking a slightly different route to the post office or deciding to drop in to the library on a whim could seem like an outrageous indulgence.

As I walked home with the paper tucked under one arm, I nodded a hello to one of the neighbours. I didn't know the man's name, but he had the look of a fellow widower about him. Not quite ashen, but certainly desaturated to a degree. The haircut three weeks overdue and a scrap of tissue paper to heal a shaving wound. It was only a matter of time before his spectacles would be held together with a sticking plaster at the bridge. I liked to think that I was holding it together more successfully than most, but it was impossible to see oneself through a stranger's eyes. Two teenage girls walked past me on the pavement, one recounting a piece of gossip breathlessly, the other listening intently to every word. To them I was completely invisible. A non-person. Had it only been forty years ago that I had returned to this town as a handsome, decorated war hero? I'd helped secure the freedom that these youngsters take for granted, with my own blood and sweat. The tears I tended not to think about.

At the top of the stairs, I was about to put the key in the door when I noticed a brown-paper package on the doormat. I carried it inside and set it down beside my newspaper and milk on the Formica kitchen table. A typewritten address label and postmark. Three stamps. No one sent me things in the post any more. This would be interesting. I ripped the brown paper to reveal a small cigar box inside. No accompanying letter. Gingerly, I opened the box to reveal a mass of sawdust with a shape in the middle. At first, I didn't realise what I was looking at. And then, with a start, I discerned the corpse of a tiny bird. A featherless chick with huge eyes, only an inch or two long.

My heart was thumping in my chest as I sat down. Firstly, there was the shock of receiving such a macabre gift. But there was something else. An early memory. When I was about six years old, I found a dead chick in the garden, probably fallen from a nest. It fascinated and disturbed me greatly, this little alien form – other-worldly and grotesque. I ran to my mother who came to inspect the creature and gently explained that the poor little thing had lost its life. Something inside me died in that instant. A realisation that all living things are vulnerable to death. No soul was immune from its cold grasp. Six years of innocence evaporated in a moment, to be replaced with a lifetime of questions.

It was a tasteless prank. And the coincidence with my childhood memory simply added salt to the wound. I thought of the two girls I had passed in the street. And the old neighbour. Who could be capable of such a thing? What had I done to warrant such an unpleasant surprise? Bastards. I folded the brown paper packaging and placed it in my pocket.

I didn't want to dispose of the bird in the wastebin for some reason. I decided to take it, still in its little coffin, to the local park and set it under some bushes where it would no doubt become a meal for a fox or a crow. As I was standing up again, brushing the sawdust off my coat, a mother with a youngster walked past and gave me a disapproving look. "Come along now, Robbie, don't dawdle," she said to the boy. The boy looked fixedly into the bushes over his shoulder as he was dragged along by his mother.

I walked home via the regional post office with the empty cigar box in my coat pocket. Waiting in the queue, I became dimly aware that I would be attended to by either a young lady or a middle-aged man, depending on how long each customer took to finish their business. I had hoped it would be the young lady with the warm smile but it was the man who called out, "Next customer please" when I had finally reached the front of the line.

"What can I do for you today, sir?" he said with little

enthusiasm. His top button was undone and his tie was loosened, giving him the air of one who was failing to cope with his workload. He was wearing a very poor wig made of a cheap, shiny plastic weave. At the parting, the net fabric was clearly visible. The man had a completely smooth, pale complexion and no eyebrows whatsoever.

"I received a package today and wondered if there was any way to find out who sent it to me."

The man looked at me blankly from behind his thick-lensed spectacles.

"There's no return address, but there is a postmark. See?"

I passed the neatly folded sheet of brown paper with the stamps and postmark across the counter for the man to study. The part of his face where the eyebrows should have been rose up, and the hairpiece moved unnaturally backwards on his scalp.

"Well, that's a curious thing," he said, pushing his spectacles up and grabbing a jeweller's eyeglass from a drawer beneath the counter. He brought the brown paper close to his hugely magnified eye before sniffing loudly and passing the scrap of paper back across the counter.

"That," he said, "is a vintage postmark, no longer in common use. I think someone with an eye for antiques is pulling your leg. Your package did not come through any modern sorting office and was not delivered by the Royal Mail. Someone appears to have gone to the trouble of hand-delivering your item and stamping it with a 60-year-old frank.'"

"Really?" I said.

"Really. Queer as a nine bob note, eh? Now, is there anything else I can help you with today, sir?"

As the sun began to go down, I walked home in an unusual frame of mind. I felt as though I had been the victim of a burglary. Something had been stolen, but I wasn't quite sure what. I occasionally glanced over my shoulder, half-hoping to see someone following me. I made an impromptu visit to the library and signed out a non-fiction book about the history of the Royal Mail. Arriving home, I heated some baked beans on the hob, staring into the pot as I idly stirred, lost in thoughts of my childhood. After dinner, I placed the empty cigar box on the mantelpiece.

The next morning, there was another package on the doormat when I returned from the shops. For some peculiar reason, I suspected there might be another delivery but it was still an unpleasant jolt to see it lying there. I hurried inside as quickly as I could, my haste inspired by both anticipation and an unusual and unwelcome sense of prickly shame. Once again, I sat at the kitchen table and carefully opened the brown paper, setting it aside for forensic inspection at my leisure. Today's gift was an ancient periodical devoted to model-making. I recognised this exact issue immediately, like an old friend who hadn't aged. I turned the pages carefully, like a museum curator, to reveal various articles about the construction of balsa wood boats and aircraft, with detailed diagrams and the occasional photographic plate. Towards the end of the publication, there was a section devoted to classified advertisements for various scale model kits. One of the more prominent images showed a Greek ship from the Trojan Wars. A commercial artist had been commissioned to illustrate a Greek warrior with a shield and sword standing beside a beautiful woman in a deliberately low-cut tunic dress, her curling hair cascading down her shoulders.

At the age of ten or eleven, I had owned this very magazine and had developed somewhat of a fixation for the Greek woman. She had awoken something inside of me that was not quite sexual in nature – more of a longing to be older, to leave childhood behind and embrace my adult potential. Like the dead bird, it was another significant turning point in my life, although one I rarely thought about and not one I ever remembered mentioning to another soul. Could I have disclosed this information to a schoolfriend? Or an army chum? Someone from the office? I really didn't think so.

A thorough inspection of the brown paper with my magnifying glass revealed nothing. The same stamps, typewritten label and out-dated postmark. I was at a loss for answers, or even questions for that matter.

The next four days continued in the same vein. A vinyl recording of the piano piece that had been playing on the hospital wireless at the exact moment of my mother's death. A cricket ball, identical to the one owned by my father as a child and passed on to me with great ceremony. I had lost it the following day at school when an older boy had snatched the ball and tossed it far over my head, across the quad, over the perimeter hedge, into a neighbouring garden, never to be seen again. A photograph of a modest holiday home in the countryside behind Villefranche-sur-Mer on the Côte d'Azur. When we were camping one year near Nice, Jean had arranged to view the property with an eye to purchasing it as an investment and eventually a retirement home. I had talked her out of the idea. A pair of jade earrings. The same ones my daughter Philippa had been wearing on the day she set off for her new life in Ireland. The day that, for me, marked the beginning of a deep depression brought on by feelings of redundancy, regret and inadequacy.

By the end of the week, I had amassed a little shrine of items on the mantel. Death. Desire. Loss. Guilt. Regret. Solitude. The little bird had most likely been consumed back into nature by now. Its cigar box acted as a reminder of what once was, but was no more.

I had a premonition that there would be one, final package. Somehow, seven seemed like an appropriate tally. I also knew this final item would be different in some respect. Something that not even I had appreciated at the time.

After breakfast, I took a walk to the newsagency as usual and then came home via the park. There was a bandstand at one end and a war memorial in pale stone at the other. I walked towards the memorial and stood in front of it, admiring its tall simplicity and symmetry, but also feeling a sense of confrontation towards it. This static, sleek, beautiful piece of masonry was so far removed from my own experiences of war, it was hard to see any connection. The Roman lettering spelled out 'Dulce et decorum est pro patria mori' in graceful serifs, the u's replaced with v's. Like a secret code. An enigma. Only something that certain people of a certain age or a certain class or a certain gender could decipher. And, even then, it was still unclear what to feel. Was it sweet and fitting to die for one's country? Or was this an ironic statement? Was it a piece of rhetoric used by Roman commanders to justify their empire building? Or were these, after all, just pretty words to help keep reality at bay? I had an urge to salute the memorial, but decided against it. I walked home with barely a thought in my mind. Temporarily an automaton, empty of freewill, simply following orders.

The final package was sitting neatly on the doormat. As soon as I picked it up, from its weight and dimensions I knew what would be inside. At the kitchen table, I removed the brown paper to reveal a rusty tin box with flaking green paint and the regimental coat of arms embossed into the lid. I sat back and lit a cigarette, staring at the box for a long time.

After my injury in France during the war, my kit had been packed up by someone else and forwarded to the hospital a week later. Most of my gear was in a terrible state, but it was all there. Everything with the exception of the tin box I kept my letters in. Letters I had received from home, and letters I was in the process of writing.

Like anyone, the war had changed me in ways that I barely appreciated. I had signed up as an impressionable youth looking for adventure and I returned home wounded and with a head full of nightmares. I had been forced to confront what it means to have a stranger attempt to end one's life. To extinguish all of one's hopes and dreams. All of those years yet to be lived. All of those moments yet to be savoured. And, in equal measure, I had been forced to confront what I was capable of doing in order to safeguard my life. The unspeakable horrors that had been committed in the name of self-preservation. These things were inconsequential in comparison to the lofty notions of a common good and a just cause. But, in personal terms, they were so massive that it was simply impossible to view them in their entirety. One could only glimpse parts, and usually only in the dead of night. Surprising, unwelcome, confusing, abstracted.

Had it all been worth it? The sacrifices made in the name of preservation? Had I made the most of the mortal time I had wrestled back from the brink of extinction? I weighed up my humdrum existence of baked beans and cigarettes and park benches and newspapers. I thought of the teenagers in the street, oblivious to my shambling, grey figure. I thought of the holiday home that Jean had never enjoyed.

I walked across to the fireplace and picked up the mantel clock to make room for the tin box, setting it carefully in the centre of the now complete shrine of memories. As I finished another cigarette, I looked down at the clock in my hand. All those hours, all those minutes. A lifetime spent chasing the ever-turning hands as they endlessly sped round and round and round.

I put the clock in the sitting room sideboard, out of sight and out of mind, behind Jean's old typewriter. I opened a window to let some air in and stood looking out across the grey rooftops at the overcast sky. A feeling of calm resolution washed over me and I exhaled slowly, closing my eyes.

I hadn't opened the tin box, but I knew there would be time enough for that – in this life or the next – if I ever felt ready to do so. I knew it would contain heartache and hope, resolutions and questions, and the unbearable visions of lives that could have been, but weren't. There was no rush to discover these hidden truths. I resolved to take each day as it came. Make the most of each moment.

When I reopened my eyes, I noticed a tiny bird had landed on the window sill. It let out a chirp before flying off. I watched it for as long as I could, rising higher, before it disappeared from view. Out of sight, out of mind.

The Chair

John Prior stands at the lathe outside his workshop, pumping the flat pedal with his right foot, connected by a length of twine to the long spruce pole bouncing up and down behind and above him. He focuses all his attention on the dowel attached to the twine and held in its cradle directly in front of him, watching it accelerate first one way, then the other, in a blur of rotation, alternating between using the gouge and the chisel to release the form from within the wood. A simple chair leg, one of four, identical to its three brothers.

The noise of the gathering crowd in the village green is building, and the top of the bonfire can just be seen above the rooftop of Ruth Harper's place across the way. But John is too busy to notice these things. He has an important job to do. A proper commission for the clergyman, and he needs to focus on the matter at hand.

"You not coming, John Prior?" says Ed Barnes as he stumbles hurriedly past the lathe, ale splashing from the tankard in his hand. John looks up, but doesn't make any comment. John is a big man, perhaps the biggest in the village. If he doesn't want to share the time of day with his neighbours, or take part in the village proceedings, he doesn't, and no one ever tells him different.

After a few more families pass by, John realises he is alone with his work. Everyone else in the village is at the green, and the distant voice of the minister can be heard delivering whatever wisdom he sees fit to deliver in that endless monotone. An unemotional vessel, simply here to carry out the work of the Lord.

Young Mary Hopkins has been found guilty of consorting with the devil and is to meet her end this afternoon. Earlier that summer, Luke Watson had fallen ill with the pox and died within a matter of days, despite being the picture of health and only nineteen summers old. It transpired that Mary had been the agent of the young man's sudden demise, for reasons yet unclear, despite her protestations that she and Luke were in love and he had asked for her hand in marriage secretly just a week before his death. But there was clear evidence of sorcery and magic about the girl, having been spied in the north woods conversing with spirits, mumbling incantations and collecting all kinds of weird botanical ingredients for ungodly and unnatural purposes.

The witness to these crimes was none other than John Prior who had no option but to relate all he had seen to the clergyman, just a few days hence, having struggled with his own conscience for a week or so. He feels now that his duty has been done. Having a witch within the village is no good for anyone, risking spoiled crops, disease, nightmarish visions, pestilence and God only knows what else. So, in his mind, he feels satisfied he has done the right thing.

There is a sudden cheer from the crowd. Again, John ignores the sounds and carries on with his work, turning the wooden dowel back and forth, pumping the footboard, up and down.

The north woods had indeed been the scene of an unspeakable act, but not as John Prior had related it. For it was there that he had lured one of the village children, little Noah Hastings, under the pretext of hunting for wild boar, only to grab him most violently and perform dreadful things under the devilish spell of his darkest passions. Poor Mary Hopkins, collecting wildflowers, had stumbled onto the scene, instantly taking in its full meaning, before running back to her home as fast as she could. Despite her silence, John Prior had decided to take no chances. Of course, once accused, Mary began to relate the story of her woodland encounter to her accusers. But, by then, her testimony sounded sour, like someone gasping for air as they drowned. And petrified little Noah Hastings was mute on the subject, no doubt fearful for his own soul.

And so it was agreed that Mary Hopkins' short life of fifteen years should be ended, and may God have mercy on her soul.

As the fire begins to crack and pop and the smoke rises over the rooftops, John resumes his work with renewed vigour, the rhythmic scraping of the chisel helping to drown out the sound of the blaze. But he cannot ignore the piercing dreadful song of the girl screaming as she is cleansed from this world. A sound so high in its pitch and so disquietingly inhuman, that it beggars belief. Perhaps she truly is an agent of the supernatural after all? The noises of the crowd turn from accusation, to celebration, to pity, to fear, before dwindling to silence. Only the scream now, travelling through the late summer air and gently brushing up against the blade of the chisel, carving a microscopic record of Mary's last moments into the tiny groove-like indentations in the wood.

And then, the palpable relief that there is only the sound of the burning fire. A soul departed. Slowly, John Prior brings the lathe to a standstill. He is spent, beads of sweat on his brow. He stares at the chair leg before him for a long time, until the villagers begin to disperse from the green, back to their homes and their work, back to their lives. Satisfied that justice has been served in the eyes of the Lord, and arguably more God-fearing than they had been upon waking that morning. The witch would have no funeral and no grave, and let that be a lesson to us all. Ed Barnes walks past John Prior without so much as a second glance, rubbing soot from his cheek.

Once assembled, the set of two chairs are clad in intricate leatherwork by Matthew Partridge, a travelling artisan, eccentric in nature and rumoured to secretly hold pagan beliefs. Each chair features an identical design – the round face of a bearded man, not unlike a sun god or green man. At first, John Prior is apprehensive that the clergyman would have some misgivings about the artistry, but the pastor is delighted. "A fine and accurate countenance of the Lord Himself, John." They are outstanding pieces of furniture, perfectly finished with brass studs, varnished to a deep, smooth chestnut, and upholstered with the best hide available this season. Once installed on either side of the humble altar in St Michael's church, they appear like royal thrones to the village folk. A fearful symbol of power and affluence, the two unblinking bearded faces keeping a watchful eye over their flock. A theatrical flourish that seems to elevate the small church to the status of a cathedral.

Over the decades, John Prior attends the regular Sunday services and admires his handiwork. Although, there is always the grim feeling that the chair on the left – for he knew with certainty it is that one – is somehow imbued faintly with the spirit of the young witch. A cold breath strokes the back of his neck when he considers this notion, before pushing it deep inside his soul, where it mingles with the multitude of conflicting ideas and disturbing thoughts that he has made it his life's work to suppress.

As an older man, he meets his end one day, aptly, whilst walking in the north woods collecting timber. He trips over a root and cracks his skull open on a rock, like an egg. At least that's what most people believe when his body is found some days later. Only young Noah Hastings knows better, now a man himself, shy and quiet in his nature, but powerfully built. And when John Prior makes his final journey to the afterlife, and the clergyman talks at length about his good standing as a vital and upright member of their small community, Noah can swear that the leather face on the church's western altar chair takes on an unusual expression as a cloud flits across the morning sun. An expression of grim satisfaction mixed with subtle fury.

Yet more seasons came and went. John Prior's lathe and tools had long been taken to pieces and given to the smith, who had melted the various parts down to create tools, stirrups, pokers, pots, kettles. The kettle would scream every time it boiled. The chisel used to create the church chairs lay in the corner of the smith's forge until there was a request from the clergyman to create a wrought iron gate for the church. The metal blade was smelted down and mixed with a multitude of other scrap to form the basis of the gate, which was installed in the autumn. In later years, a row of iron railings was established around the full perimeter of the church grounds, to segregate the holy land from the common.

The sun spun around the world and the world of mankind changed at an ever-increasing pace. Men perished in wars, harvests were collected, babies were born, saints and sinners went about their business. And, all the time, the two altar chairs with their stoic faces stood witness to the christenings, funerals and sermons of the village. The stories retold time and again from the pulpit were constant, offering solace to some and anxiety to others. One day, a visiting bishop sat on the right-hand chair and it collapsed unexpectedly under his weight. It was pronounced beyond repair due to an infestation of woodworm, and was unceremoniously thrown on a bonfire, leaving its twin alone in the world. It was felt that the lone chair now looked out of place in the church, creating an unsettling sinister asymmetry, and so it was placed in one of the small private rooms behind the altar, hidden from view. Over the years, it bore silent witness to many unsettling acts of intimidation, humiliation and depravity, carried out in secret against the innocents of the parish and always with the excuse that the Lord's will was being interpreted expertly and carried out to the letter in whatever way the clergyman saw fit.

More generations came and went and, although the world became unrecognisably faster and noisier outside the railings of St Michael's, the dusty atmosphere of incantations, scents and ancient rituals changed little within the hallowed walls of the little church. The chair with the godlike face sat on its patch of red carpet in the darkness and stillness of its tiny room, the four legs fashioned by John Prior bearing the weight of centuries of existence.

One day, a group of workmen in overalls arrived at the church and worked solidly for two days removing the wrought iron gates, smoking cigarettes and making crude jokes under their breaths about the clergyman and the cloud of rumours that surrounded him. The iron was noisily stacked on the back of a flatbed lorry and driven off to a factory, where it was smelted down in an industrial furnace, an inferno of hellish temperatures. The molten metal was poured into moulds to create the cylindrical casings of incendiary shells. When finished, the shells were stacked in their batteries, shining darkly in the gloom, waiting to play their part in the war effort, raining down destruction upon the citizens of faraway cities.

Some months later, a cluster of shells was carefully loaded into a bomber, whose propellers noisily carried it into the twilight air above the hedgerows, making its way east to suck the very life and air from a city through the sheer force of fire. As the bomber cruised over the rural landscape of its homeland, one of its young and inexperienced crewmen made the fatal error of accidentally releasing part of the deadly payload over a small village. A single shell dropped from the aircraft, beginning its fall horizontally before gradually and inevitably pointing its nose towards the ground.

The clergyman in St Michael's had been inserting the next day's set of hymn and psalm numbers into their ornate display, aware of the sound of the bomber flying overhead, its engine noise identifying it as friend rather than foe. So, when the noise of the falling shell became distantly apparent, it came as a shock to the minister, who quickly gathered up his vestments and ran through the candlelit aisle towards the back room where the tiny trapdoor to the underground cellar was located. When he reached the door of the room, he pushed with all his might against it, but it would not budge. Unseen, on the other side of the door, a chair had somehow fallen back against the door handle, jamming it shut. Over the next five seconds, the whistling sound of the shell grew to an intense crescendo, culminating in a blinding flash of light and the sound of biblical thunder being unleashed from the very gates of hell.

Throughout the night, the fire brigade, the ARP wardens and local volunteers fought to bring the conflagration under control. But, by morning, it was clear the church was a complete ruin, with the exception of a few artefacts that had been curiously spared by the blast and subsequent inferno, including an unusual leather-bound chair that had fallen through a trapdoor and into the safety of the basement. In addition, the local police were called to investigate the fact that the basement contained a safe that had been blown apart – a safe holding a large number of distressingly candid photographs, publications of an obscene nature and even artefacts that were allegedly tools of the occult. The charred remains of the clergyman were found, in two pieces, at opposite ends of the ruined building, his blackened head twisted upwards into a silent and eternal rictus. To avoid any scandal, the contents of the basement safe were burned and no more was ever said on the matter. When the war finished, the church sold the land to a local businessman and a small petrol station and garage now stands on the formerly consecrated site.

The altar chair ended up in the hands of a local schoolteacher called Hastings, who immediately recognised both its historical significance and exquisite craftsmanship. After some remedial work to its leatherwork and some careful polishing to bring out the lustre in the woodwork, he donated the chair to a young war widow who had recently moved to the area from the city, after purchasing a pleasant tumbledown cottage on the edge of the village green. It was a happy, sunny home filled with the laughter of two young children and the bark of a collie. The chair sat in a corner of the stone-flagged kitchen and bore witness to all the lively comings and goings of the family. Twice a year, in spring and autumn, the late evening sunlight fell through the kitchen windows directly onto the image of the bearded man fashioned into the leatherwork. In the yellow light, with motes of dust and pollen swirling in the air, it sometimes looked as if the face was smiling. A beatific, serene smile earned through the wisdom and contentment of resolution.

Cast iron railings,
By the parish pastures,
Melted down,
To make tanks and Lancasters.

To their previous lives,
They cling with persistence,
With only holes in the ground,
To prove their existence.

The Hotel

This is the life I want. I try to imagine how we must look when viewed from the roadside. A bright red, open-topped car with shiny chrome bumpers. A man driving, dark hair, American sunglasses. A woman in the passenger seat, headscarf, pink lipstick, American sunglasses. A tan leather suitcase strapped to the luggage rack on the boot. AA badge and GB plate. The visceral roar of the engine.

I catch my reflection in the door mirror. The freckles on my skin remind me of the shell of an egg. The sunlight here is different to back home. More yellow. More mellow. And the sky is a different shade of blue. The poplar trees at the side of the road cast deep blue shadows – that never happens at home. We haven't seen a cloud in the sky since we drove onto the ferry at Southampton on Monday. I don't ever want to arrive, I just want to keep going and going. This is the life I want.

I met Jim two years ago at a party and we were married six months later. We make such a lovely couple. That's what everyone tells us. And it's true. Jim is fast becoming the rising star of his dealership. 'Silver Jim' they call him. I can afford to splash out on new clothes whenever I want. Jim likes me to look nice. We have friends. A social life. A flat. All the modern things that our parents didn't have.

And now we can tell everyone we've been on a driving holiday to the South of France. Technically, it's a work trip, delivering the MG to an ex-pat in Perpignan. But the photos we take won't reveal that this is someone else's car. This is our moment in the sun.

Jim pats my knee and points at a roadsign. This is our code for me to check the map. It's hard to talk above the engine noise and the wind, so we've created our own set of signals. We make a good team. Unlike many couples, we don't argue over map-reading. I'm much better at geography than Jim anyway. I like to plan our routes in pencil at breakfast, converting the inches into miles and the miles into hours. It runs like clockwork. Yes, we make a good team. We should take up rally driving.

I indicate that we need to take a left turn. It's mid-afternoon and we have plans to stay at a country hotel this evening. We deliver the car tomorrow evening and will stay in Perpignan for two nights before taking the train back to Calais. But tonight is ours. Tonight we can pretend the car belongs to us and we regularly stay in French country hotels. Was it only a few years ago I worked as a shop girl on Saturdays at Millet's fishmongers on Clark Street? If only old Mr Millet could see me now. We must look like movie stars, Jim and I.

Mid-afternoon becomes late-afternoon. The quality of the sunlight gradually softens as we drive for miles along a straight, flat road flanked by fields. We rarely see another vehicle. A tractor. A cute little Citroën van. A competition cyclist in colourful gear. Eventually, we see a sign for the village where the hotel is located. We picked it from the map this morning purely because it was halfway to Perpignan. I thrill at the thought of seeing the Mediterranean tomorrow. I've been fantasising about seeing the famous azure waters for weeks. Tonight, on the other hand, is a blank page waiting to be written.

Jim changes down to second gear as we pass the sign marking the entrance to the village. We roll slowly through the main street, which is no more than a collection of a dozen or so buildings with a small *église* at one end. The place is deserted apart from a group of swarthy looking children standing in the tiny playground of the *école primaire*. They stare at us as we drive past, unsmiling, their eyes hidden by shadows in the strong sunlight. I'm tempted to stick out my tongue at them, but decide against it. There's something unsettling about the way they look at us. They are regarding us. Evaluating us. *Nous vous regardons*. We represent something they find foreign and distasteful. Arrogance. Affluence. Otherness. There is a cold, detached quality to the way they gaze endlessly. We drive on but, looking in the door mirror, I notice the children have ambled into the middle of the road to continue staring at us as we depart. Jim looks at me over his sunglasses and raises an eyebrow.

"The locals seem very... local," Jim says, grinning. It makes me giggle. He accelerates the car through the village, taking us towards its outskirts.

We drive along a tree-lined avenue towards the hotel, the car's wheels crunching on the gravel. It's a rustic building with green shutters, the walls covered in mass of overgrown ivy. It should be 'charming', but there's something a little off about the proportions. Humble, but with ideas above its station. After parking up, we both struggle a little to unfold and reconnect the car's leather roof. I notice a very old Frenchwoman dressed in black, her grey hair in a bun, sitting on a little wooden seat among some trees at the side of the hotel. She's looking at us intently with an expression that's hard to discern. Her eyes are screwed up tightly and her mouth is grinning widely, revealing a toothless smile. But it's hard to know if she's aware of us at all. I get the impression she might be blind. As Jim grabs the suitcase with both hands and we make our way towards the reception, she says something in French to herself. I catch a word that sounds like *viande* or *vieille*. The cicadas sing loudly, just to remind us that we're not in England any more. I remember a piece of French folklore from school: the cicadas were sent by God to disrupt the peasants' endless siestas and stop them from growing lazy.

Walking inside, it takes a moment for our eyes to adjust to the darkness. The walls are clad in heavy wood panels. The ebony floor is shiny. There's a smell of linseed in the air, mixed with something else – a faintly foetid, outdoor smell. A family of four adults and four children are checking out, talking rapidly in French. They are all remarkably similar looking, with slightly hunched postures and flat, wide, moonlike faces. I hazard a guess they are perhaps aunts, uncles, nephews and nieces. One of the children is a pretty young girl of about twelve years of age, who looks entirely different to the others. Different posture, different face, different skintone. As the family noisily exit the hotel, laden with luggage, the girl glances towards me with an expression of heartbreaking sorrow. It sends a little chill down my spine.

Jim pings the bell on the counter and we both straighten up a little, conscious that we will be evaluated soon enough. We have nothing to hide now, as a married couple. But it wasn't that long ago we were checking in to guest houses as Mr & Mrs Smith-Jones. I feel a strange pang of guilt as the family outdoors start the engine to their station wagon and drive away.

A door behind the reception counter opens a little, revealing a small office. A large, balding man dressed in a string vest and dark trousers holds the door ajar. He is looking at a transistor radio in his hand, a cream coloured earpiece in one ear. The tinny sound of a sports commentary can just about be heard coming from the radio. He does not acknowledge our presence in the slightest. He appears to be transfixed, staring intently at the tuning dial. Without any warning, he swears very loudly in French and slams the transistor down on a bureau table, the earpiece flying. He closes his eyes and lets out a long sigh. He presses his palms to his face and swears again, this time more slowly and quietly. Bringing his hand down, he appears to notice us for the first time. He makes no effort to approach the counter. I get the distinct impression he is blaming us for whatever misfortune his team has just experienced.

"*Parlez-vous anglais, monsieur?*" I say, as pleasantly as I can. Jim doesn't speak a word of French. He 'did woodwork' instead. So I have become our official translator. Jim looks after all things mechanical and physical, like carrying bags and filling petrol tanks. I'm in charge of language, navigation and currency, which is actually very liberating.

"*Non,*" says the man in the string vest, bluntly. He offers no indication that he can help us in any way.

After a brief pause, I adopt what I like to call my regal stance. It's a little trick I learned a few years ago. In my mind, I pretend that I'm a junior member of the royal family. Not a princess, but some regional baroness or duchess. Something believable. And then I simply act accordingly. Tradespeople are there to be gently kept in line. I believe it's quite acceptable to make the other 'gals' in the typing pool feel inferior, in a very polite way of course. And saying just the right things in a slightly more refined accent helps one to fit in with one's would-be peers. All this despite the fact that I grew up in a very humble terraced house with parents who regularly dropped their aitches. It's amazing what one can pick up from listening carefully to the wireless and making notes at the pictures. Class, despite what people think, can be learned quite easily.

"*Écoutez, s'il vous plait,*" I begin, fixing the bald man with a clear and emotionless gaze. The man's demeanour changes just a little. Just enough to confirm a minor victory on my part. I ask the man for a double room for one night and enquire about breakfast in my best French, but delivered through the lens of my hoighty-toighty BBC accent (which is no mean feat, if I do say so myself).

The man runs a hand across his shining pate before turning to take a key from a hook board on the wall behind him.

"*Petit déjeuner, neuf heures. Chambre six.*" He passes the key across the counter, leans forward and points along a murky hallway towards a stairwell.

"*Merci beaucoup*," I say as I pick up the key, but the man has already retreated into his office and is stuffing the earpiece from his transistor back into his ear. The door slowly swings shut.

The staircase has a threadbare carpet with a *fleur de lys* pattern. Unusually, the steps turn first to the left, then upwards, then to the right, then upwards again onto a small landing. I hear Jim struggling with the suitcase behind me, muttering something under his breath. The landing leads to a poky hall with two doors. The hall appears to have been built at a different scale to the rest of the house, as if for smaller people. Everything is still in proportion, but at least a tenth smaller. The ceiling is at a steep angle, following the roofline, and a tiny skylight projects a rhombus of sun onto the opposite wall, the beam filled with swirling golden dust. One of the doors is blank, the other has a brass number six. I place the heavy key in the lock and open the door, realising that I'll have to stoop a little to avoid bumping my head on the doorframe. Jim isn't so careful and I hear a hollow cranial thump behind me followed by an irritable, "Damn and blast!"

I'd been hoping for a quaintly rustic farmhouse room with a view of rolling countryside. Maybe some vineyards. Maybe a water jug and bowl instead of a sink. The reality is a disappointment. I don't know why I'm surprised. It is the destiny of most hotel rooms to let their occupants down. It's a small, plain room with a chest of drawers, a dressing table (no mirror), a lumpy bed and a cloakroom sink (which needs a good clean). Jim flops onto the bed with a sigh as I sit on the edge. I try not to let my disappointment show. He holds my hand for a moment and I feel a little better. The air in the room is hot and heavy. I open the window, pushing open the shutters to reveal a view of a wall, just a few feet away. I pop my head outside and look to the right, along a kind of alcove in the architecture, where I can just about see some greenery and the edge of a blue swimming pool.

Pulling the suitcase onto the bed, I hold up my new one-piece swimming costume in front of me.

"*Piscine?*" I say with a smirk, cheering myself up.

Jim looks at me quizzically. "I beg your pardon?"

It takes a while to find the pool, dressed in our swimming gear with bath towels wrapped around us. We make our way through the deserted reception area on tip-toe for some reason, giggling quietly. Outside, we go around the side of the building (the old lady has vanished), through the trees and eventually find the pool. There is an unsettling green-brown tide mark around the edge at water level, and a few leaves and insects floating in the water. I climb gingerly down the rickety ladder and discover that the water is cool but entirely bearable. Jim starts to swim laps while I tread water at the deep end, turning my face to the sun and closing my eyes behind my sunglasses. I want to relax and enjoy the moment, but the water feels greasy somehow, as if there is a microbial layer of oil on the surface. I desperately wanted this moment to be different. A snapshot of me splashing in sparkling water. Look how healthy and attractive and wealthy and stylish and happy we are! Don't you just want to be here? Wouldn't you give everything to be me? In reality, I had an unexpected wave of homesickness. A sense of ennui that made me long for my childhood home, the games we played in the garden when I was a six-year-old, the innocence, the simplicity of living. Fairies, pixies, puppies and kittens. I'm curiously tired of the responsibility of living up to my own aspirations.

There is a dull thump in the trees to one side of the pool. Jim looks at me for a moment and then climbs out of the pool to investigate. He walks a few paces and then stops, grimacing at the ground.

"What is it?" I call out. He doesn't answer for a second.

"Dead bird. Poor thing's a bit of a mess. Shall we go in?"

There's a shared bathroom at the end of our hallway, but we appear to be the only residents in the hotel so we can treat it like our own. After a soak in the tub, I put on the dress with the graphic print that cost a small fortune from the new boutique in Farnham Street. I attach a pair of false lashes that make me look like Twiggy. Jim's reading one of his Alistair MacLean novels on the bed while I get ready.

"Do you think I'll be okay without a tie tonight, darling?" he asks.

"You'll be arriving in a bright red MG with me at your side. I don't think anyone is going to notice what you have or haven't got around your neck."

We drive for twenty minutes into a nearby market town, which seems like a metropolis compared to the village. The sun is very low in the sky and the air is cooler. It feels much more like a holiday now. I feel happy. We park in a cobbled street just off the main square and sit down on the terrace of the first restaurant we come to. There's a sense of timeless joy to the square. Old men playing boules. A young couple on a *promenade*. A woman walking her tiny dog. Piano music coming from an upstairs apartment. Teenagers on scooters tooting their horns. A man walks past the MG and stops to admire it from various angles, peering through the side window at the cockpit. I can tell Jim is infuriated that he's unable to go over and talk to the man about horsepower and gear ratios in French.

I order two steaks (well done for me, rare for Jim) and a bottle of the house red. The waiter is the real deal – serious, immaculate, courteous to a fault, completely absorbed in the world of food and drink.

We wait for the food to arrive and enjoy watching this pretty little corner of the world go about its evening business, settling down for the night. I marvel at my fortunes. From lanky schoolgirl to shy shopgirl to typist to office administrator to international traveller in just seven years. There was a feeling that the best was yet to come, too. The world was changing. Vibrant clothes, music, art, ideas. New opportunities for the new generation. New opportunities for women that my mother simply cannot comprehend. Money, technology, convenience, speed. We are the masters of the universe with the future in our hands. This is the life I want.

Returning with the steaks, the waiter tells me that my husband is very lucky to have such a beautiful car, but it's like an old farmer's jalopy compared to his beautiful wife. I thank him graciously and then translate the compliment to Jim. Jim smiles and says it's funny how no man would get away with making a comment like that in England but, in France, it seems to be part of the normal order of things. I realise that this little incident may well become part of our personal shared history as a couple. Part of the cement that keeps any relationship together. I imagine myself, perhaps ten years from now, telling the story at a dinner party. Jim and I looking tenderly at one another, being the only two witnesses to the event. The story will have been told many times by then, and it will feel like a script. Me hoping that he still finds me more beautiful than the car. Jim making a joke that, as he doesn't understand French, the waiter could have been saying anything. Everyone laughs. In my imagination, the house we are in is very chic and modern, with a long well-tended garden. We're all drinking champagne. There are two angelic children in bed upstairs, a boy and a girl.

By the time we order coffee, the sun has set and the little town square is illuminated with pretty strings of lights. The bells of the clock tower strike ten. I ask for the bill and leave a generous tip. As we get up to leave, our waiter gives us a theatrical bow and bids us farewell. Walking across the square with my arm linked through Jim's, he places the car keys in my hand.

"Do you mind driving, darling? Tiny bit squiffy and wouldn't want to scratch the paintwork."

Behind the steering wheel, I adjust the mirror and wiggle the gear stick. Jim tries to give me some advice about driving on the "wrong side of the road", but I start the engine before he can finish his sentence. I know I'm a better driver than him and I think he does too.

Outside the town, I gently squeeze the throttle and feel the satisfying grip of acceleration take us into the dark country roads. Insects caught in the headlamp beams look like shooting stars. I take the corners expertly, shifting down through the gears and then up again, using the weight of the car to propel us through the curves, following a neat racing line, the engine roaring like thunder.

The hotel looms into view, a black silhouette against the twilight with a single lamp hovering over the main entrance. I remember a painting by Magritte I once saw in a magazine. I park up neatly and switch the engine and headlamps off. We sit for a moment in the darkness, listening to the clicking sounds of the metal cooling down and the faintest swish of the fuel settling in the tank. Jim leans towards me and we kiss. He tastes of wine and cigarettes. When a light goes on somewhere at the side of the building, we break away from each other and look expectantly at the corner of the building. After a while we hear the distant noise of a toilet being flushed and a door closing. The light goes off again. We get out of the car, closing the doors as quietly as we can, and tiptoe towards the front door. As an afterthought, I go back to double check that all the car doors and boot are locked. Even though Jim is only a few feet away, I don't like the feeling of being on my own and I hurry back to him as quickly as I can.

Inside, the reception area is lit by a single, weak bulb in the ceiling. There's more shadow than light. We race up the labyrinth of stairs, and both make a beeline for the shared loo. Jim manages to sneak in before me, the swine, leaving me standing outside in the hall. I can hear him peeing, a sound which seems to go on forever. As I wait, I study a framed wedding photograph on the wall of a stern looking couple from the previous century. They look miserable. The groom is standing and, for some reason, has a goose in his arms. The bride is seated in front of him, with a knife on her lap. The toilet flushes.

Jim reappears in the hallway with a wry smile on his face. He goes to peck me on the lips, but I playfully push him away on my way into the loo and lock the door behind me. Sitting down, I watch the wooden handle on the end of the lightswitch cord swinging backwards and forwards, gently knocking against the doorframe. There is a tall window behind me, the high cistern blocking the upper pane of unfrosted glass. I feel a wave of unease as I imagine the illuminated window as seen from the trees outside. A bright yellow rectangle in the darkness with the smudged head and shoulders of a female silhouette framed neatly at the base. A moth bumps into the glass as I lean forward to switch off the light. I finish washing my hands in darkness with the plumbing shuddering like an irate walking stick banging on a ceiling.

Back in the sanctuary of our room, Jim is asleep on top of the covers, sprawled across his side of the bed in just his vest and undershorts. The day has finally caught up with him, sitting behind the wheel, the fresh country air, a hearty meal, and, mostly, the wine. I go through the reassuring routine of carefully removing my make-up and clothing, applying skin cream, brushing my teeth and getting into my nightdress (the simple, comfortable one as opposed to the yet-to-be-worn lace one purchased specifically for this trip). I climb into bed beside the invisible sounds of Jim's breathing and allow my head to sink into the pillow, waiting for my dreams to carry me gently from the realm of the conscious into the uncharted waters of deep sleep. Sinking through disjointed imagery of poplar trees and waiters, steering wheels and children's faces. Waiting for the sleep narrative to arrive and write me into its story without my permission.

A phone starts to ring. It sounds as if it is directly underneath the floor, meaning that our room must be roughly above the reception. It rings for a long time, bringing me back to full wakefulness. Jim continues to sleep, out for the count. Eventually, the noise stops, mid ring, its imagined echo reverberating silently through the house for a moment. Somehow the silence now seems different. Fragile and expectant.

I turn my head on the pillow and attempt to drift off again. I'm sinking towards sleep, but I'm engulfed by an unusual feeling that I haven't experienced since I was little girl suffering from a fever. My consciousness starts to shrink within an ever-expanding darkness. Over time, I become the size of a pea, then a pinhead, then an atom, while the darkness enlarges to the size of a stadium, a planet, an entire cosmos. It is both terrifying and exciting at the same time. I feel as if I could lose my entire being if I become any smaller, if the darkness becomes any bigger. Dwindling into nothingness. Oblivion. But, like falling under the weight of gravity, it's impossible to stop the process. It's the way things must be.

The phone rings again. Moments later? A few minutes? Half an hour? Again, the seemingly incessant ringing that dies suddenly. I get up to open the window a few inches and, back in bed, a cool layer of air caresses my face. Sleep comes a little more quickly and deeply this time. I'm in the field next to the hotel in my nightdress, searching through the long grass trying to find the keys to the car. Jim is standing with his arms outstretched, pretending to be a scarecrow. It's infuriating because he refuses to help me find the keys. He's laughing at my frustration. I stand up, filled with anger, ready to slap him across the cheek. There's a very loud flapping noise overhead. Looking up, I see a huge black crow falling from the sky directly above me, its blue-black beak gleaming sharply in the moonlight, jaws opening wide.

I wake with a start. I'm aware that it's a noise that has woken me, possibly a loud noise, but upon regaining my consciousness, all is quiet. I lie very still and listen very carefully. Jim's slow, even breathing. The quiet tick of a wristwatch. The faintest breeze from the window. And something else. Right on the very edge of my hearing. At the point, far away, where the inaudible and audible must meet. Yet unmistakable. Incredibly faint screaming. A long scream, followed by another long scream, followed by another. A mile away maybe? Or in a basement? A television set or a wireless perhaps? Surely not. Even in France the broadcasters must have concluded their programming by now. It's the dead of night, 2am by the luminous dial of my wristwatch on the lamp stand. More screaming. Tiny distant sounds. Surely, it must be an animal. Yes, a fox or a cat or a bird. Yes, it must be a…

The phone starts to ring again, loudly. I poke Jim in his side, but he's dead to the world. I feel angry for some reason. Angry at this dreadful place, and this dreadful night. Angry at Jim. Angry at that bloody phone. Ring, ring. Ring, ring. I'm thirsty so I put on Jim's jacket over my nightdress and leave the room, filled with the confidence of a sleeper who has returned to the world of reality.

I decide to go down to the breakfast room to find a glass and some drinkable water. The little light in the reception area below provides just enough illumination to help me navigate down the warren of stairs. Ring, ring. Ring, ring. Louder with every step. Reeling me in like a fish following a lure. In the reception area, the sound of the telephone is deafening. I walk towards the counter and lean over, intending to knock the handset off its cradle, ending the call, ending the noise. As I put my hand down towards the telephone it stops ringing, mid-ring, and I find myself curiously frozen, unable to move in the sudden and absolute silence. I stare at my hand in the dim light.

There is a loud click and the light is extinguished. I am in complete darkness. An immediate, animalistic sensation of terror sweeps through me. I can actually hear my heart beating through my open mouth, as tiny rapid gasps. My eyes widen. My ribcage is hammering. Muscles tense. Hairs rise up on the nape of my neck and on my forearms. My mouth goes dry. Adrenaline courses through my veins. I am attuned to the slightest change in atmosphere. Poised. Waiting.

As my pupils dilate, I can make out some detail. The blue nocturnal light entering the windows at the front of the hotel, on either side of the door. With an icy tremor I realise that the car is no longer parked where we left it.

There is a subtle noise behind me. The subtlest of noises.

The gentle tap of a rubber-soled shoe on the wooden floor. A small noise. The noise of a child. A child's footstep. And then the cold, sharp, quick pain of a metal blade entering the upper part of my back, silently slicing into my heart from behind and ending things. Swiftly. Expertly. Kindly.

A coolness spreads between my shoulder blades as my legs buckle and I fall in a heap onto the hard floor. I am unable to move, I am unable to breathe, I am losing the ability to see, my consciousness receding backwards down a telescope held the wrong way round.

I try to think, quickly. I realise this is the end and I want to make this moment count. Was this the life I really wanted? With Jim and the car and the travel and the clothes and always having to keep up appearances? Competing endlessly to prove my happiness? Would there have been children? Would they have been angels or monsters? Or something in between? Smaller versions of us, worrying about what everyone else thinks? Would a simpler life have given me more joy?

I realise I will never know. Instead, I will exist forever in this moment. The poor, pretty girl who appeared on the front page of the newspaper after her death. The girl whose life, hopes, virtues and trespasses were distributed across the nation and beyond in black-and-white grainy photographs and sensationalised tabloid storytelling. Until, naturally, the story will go cold. Yesterday's newsprint wrapped around fish and chips and then discarded into a gutter. Disintegrating in the rain. Flowing down pipes and drains, subterranean, back to the anonymity of the endless sea. I let go and realise that all my worries have dissolved into nothing and I become the very essence of peace. I no longer need to care. My destiny is no longer something I have to attend to. My options have diminished to zero. As my eyes close, I am still wondering if this is the life I want.

The Threshold

The dreams began not long after my thirty-fourth birthday, when my sister made a joke about me being fully eligible for a mid-life crisis now that I'd reached the halfway point of our father's life. He had met his end some years previously as a result of a cardiac arrest aged three score years and not-quite-ten. The comment was meant in jest, but it irked me nonetheless. How dare she? How dare she presume I was now closer to death than birth. I still felt like a young, virile man with my life ahead of me. But, the fact of the matter was, I knew in my heart that my best years were most probably behind me. My wife had divorced me. I saw my son rarely, due to both the geographical and psychological distances separating us. My business ventures seemed to always end in failure, through no fault of my own. And my soul was filling up gradually with a sense of despondency, like a bottle being filled with engine oil. Periods of exhaustion, alternated with periods of anxiety. What a joyful existence.

All my life, I'd had no trouble getting to sleep. I looked forward to bed every evening and was usually unconscious within a minute of my head hitting the pillow. With the exception of some feverish nightmares as a child, my dreams were, by and large, unremarkable. Foolish narratives about the complexities of my work and social experiences, hazy memories of school, surrealist flights of fancy in which anything was possible, the occasional erotic fantasy – sometimes enjoyable, sometimes queasy. So, the first time I dreamed of the room, it was an unexpected shock to realise that my subconscious could have such a merciless effect upon me.

The dream always begins with me arriving at a house and seeing it from a distance. Not always the same house, although often it is made of red brick. Not an opulent stately home, but a substantial suburban dwelling. The design is invariably a little askew. Unsatisfying to the eye. The house looks as if it has been added to over many years, with extensions at curious angles and a multitude of sloping rooflines, coming together in a riot of geometry. The weather is usually pleasant – wintry, cloudless blue skies with low sunlight that icily scorches the eye when looking up at the architecture. The window frames of the house have peeling white paint. There are subtle distortions in the ancient, melting glass. There is a stained glass fan light above the imposing, classic doorway. A brass knocker with a lion's head. A cast iron boot-scraper beside the top step.

Invariably, I find myself inside the building, but with no memory of a door being opened. The interior seems to bear little relation to what I saw of the exterior. It's usually darker inside, and much larger. Long, dimly lit corridors that seem to extend endlessly towards Victorian kitchens and pantries, half-viewed through half-open doors. A dusty atmosphere hangs over everything, as if the property has lain vacant for several months, or is inhabited by people who rarely move. Old portrait photographs hang on gently peeling wallpaper. Threadbare patterned carpets cling to the floorboards and wooden flights of stairs. Grey decanters hide behind the smudged glass doors of cabinets. Ancient mirrors rust and decay, half-heartedly reflecting the dim light of yellowing bulbs hidden behind nicotine-stained shades. The corpses of long-dead insects subtly decorate the corners of rooms. Through the windows, I see that day has become early evening, and the silhouetted leaves of trees sway ominously back and forth.

I'm in an upper storey now, approaching a landing where a complex negotiation of stairwells comes together. Little flights of two or three stairs each with curving bannisters, moving up and down to take one towards other landings, returns, mezzanines. Directly ahead, at the top of a short flight of stairs is a seemingly innocuous room, the door sitting ajar. It appears to be empty and silent. No carpets on the floor. A single window in the distance looking out on a blue sky – curiously daylight once again.

It's at this point that I usually become aware of my fear. A huge, overwhelming terror that is responding to something unseen within the room. A panic brought on by the realisation that whatever is in the room wishes to do me untold harm. It wants to annihilate my soul and erase all trace of my existence. It is filled with anger and hatred, aimed squarely at me – the person who has dared to trespass against it. As I approach the door, I look across at a nearby landing where a wooden box is sitting under a window. Without warning, it moves a few inches across the carpet by itself. My heart contracts in a spasm of dread. I'm aware that something is about to appear at the doorway. Stop it, now. At this point, I usually wake with a start, sitting up in bed, breathing rapidly, willing myself to regain my composure.

The unpleasantness of these dreams, and their confusing, unknown origin, meant that I was becoming more and more fretful at bedtime. Turning out the bedroom light was no longer an invitation to be carried away gently into the realm of reveries. Instead, it was like boarding a train every night that would take an ever-more circuitous route to the same awful destination.

It was a word that I tended to avoid, due to its associations with all things supernatural and religious. But, there was no other way to describe the feelings generated within these nightmares. It was a feeling of evil.

Sometimes I would be alone in the dreams. At other times, I would be accompanied by others. Character actors from school or college or work life. Why is this so? Is it because the subconscious needs to have these people witness what is happening in order to lend credibility to the story? No matter how strange the location and the narrative, it must be true because so-and-so or such-and-such is here too, and they're obviously not dreaming.

On one occasion, I was accompanied around the dream house by a shiny green salamander with comically large eyes. It constantly crept around after me, looking up, as if asking to be lifted and petted the way a puppy would, but without any trace of emotion in its eyes, its motives entirely unclear. It was not looking for affection, food, or warmth but, instead, something more blank than that. An atavistic need that was, for the moment, hidden from meaning, but darkly sinister in a cold, unfeeling way. Not unnatural, but entirely and inescapably of nature itself.

Another time, the house was filled with a grim-looking party of guests in sober attire. I ended up having an altercation with a short, sickly looking man about the fact he was being a 'nuisance'. He raised his voice in anger at my accusation, proving my point.

The more I became anxious about the dreams, which were increasing in frequency, the more I would try to find ways to explain them away. Where was this evil coming from? Inside of me, or outside of me? Were forces seen or unseen working to chip away at my integrity during daylight hours, forcing my subconscious to create phantoms to torment my sleep? I thought of the many neighbours in my street, the people across the city, the entire nation. From tiny innocents, to decrepit old souls. All of them feverishly dreaming the night away – their subconscious minds weaving so many unseen stories. A vast web of perplexing imagery and thoughts that was so very real to the dreamers, happening in every country across the globe.

And I became more aware of my subconscious playing an increasingly important role in my waking life. From dialling up memories in one's mind's eye, to projecting oneself a few hours or days into the future to make plans. Consulting mental maps when navigating city streets. Travelling to far-off countries when reading the news. Stepping inside the bodies and souls of others out of a sense of empathy, curiosity or spite. Even the simple act of reading requires that magical part of our brains to conjure up highly-detailed models of places, people and objects, filling in the gaps of our broad brush stokes with intricate penmanship. But who is holding that pen? Is it what we loosely call our soul, our mind? Does the creative intelligence lie within the nuclei of our cells, powered by our magical mitochondria – those alien symbionts that come from God only knows where?

All of this seemed to hint towards a conclusion that the subconscious was truly master of our souls and that we, the waking, were simply puppets following preordained paths imprinted upon us over millennia of evolution. And the oldest of these paths naturally made us wary and fearful of the most obvious and universal of truths – our headlong rush awards the abyss of death itself. Stop reading.

Over several months, the dreams continued. Similar locations. The final approach to an open room. The feeling of dread. They mostly followed the same cinematic structure and cliffhanger ending. Sometimes sound, music or speech would play a part. Dusty gramophone recordings heard in far off parts of the house. A mirror falling from a wall and crashing to the floor. A slim black figure glimpsed in the distance of a murky corridor, silhouetted by moonlight, standing confrontationally, staring fixedly in my direction.

Once, as I walked towards the final room, a man appeared in my path. A very ordinary, mild looking fellow in a raincoat, with a small dog on a leash. As usual, the sense of dread would build up exponentially and, in this case, the man's expression turned quickly from blank emotion to the most extreme vision of pure hatred, aimed like a beam towards me. Looking at his eyes, I had a loathsome realisation that I was, in a way, looking into a mirror somehow. Silently, the dog barked frantically and strained at its leash. No sound could be heard until the man screamed, "*This is my...*"

As I awoke, I realised that I had screamed the same three words in unison. I had heard both my voice and his voice in that fleeting moment between being asleep and being awake. It was hugely unnerving, to be aware of such a split in my being – a split between 'self' and 'other'.

This was the last dream of its kind that I experienced. For whatever reason, the recurring visits to that dreadful place ended and I was able to return, for the time being, to my normal sleep patterns. I knew that part of the puzzle lay in the fact that I never once got to travel across the threshold into that final room. I'm aware that, one day, I will have to make that fateful journey. I only hope that the grim feeling of despair is associated with the act of crossing the threshold, rather than with anything that lies within. An irrational, but timeless fear of our ultimate journey, rather than the destination to which we will all ultimately arrive.

How did this psycho-virus get into my head? My only conclusions are as follows. The dream room is a fabrication of my subconscious. I didn't render this story from my imagination, it rendered itself. In all its technicolour, horrific, terrifying glory. A million times more intense than any piece of cinematography. The same sparks of electricity between the synapses that helped me type this sentence, fired themselves into being, to will a complex and worrisome scenario into existence. A scenario that, I suppose, serves some purpose in terms of preparing me for what lies ahead.

Even typing these paragraphs has been unpleasant in and of itself. Cathartic, purgative, cleansing, but unpleasant. On rereading these pages over several drafts, I have noticed several words that seem to have been inexplicably amended and inserted without my conscious knowledge.

And now you have ingested my description of the dream house and its fearful room, it exists in your mind as well. Maybe not exactly the same, but similar in many respects. I hope your subconscious chooses to ignore it completely. But how can you? If I ask you *not* to think of an elephant, of course you can't help doing the opposite. Being only human, your mind may decree that a nocturnal visit may have some irresistible value, to prepare your waking self for all eventualities, and perhaps for the gratification and amusement of its darker parts. Two minds in one body. Two realities in one mind. Too late to stop.

Whatever the motivations of our hidden selves, at least we can rest easy that the contents of the room will always remain screened from our mortal consciousness. For the time being at least.

The Burden

"If I'm aware that I'm insane, does that mean I'm sane? I can never remember what the rule is."

The woman sitting in my office is around 35 years of age, according to her file, with unruly blue-black hair tied back in a clasp. She's wearing a grey sweater and dark jeans. Everything about her is ordinary. Ordinary sallow skin, ordinary face, ordinary looks, ordinary build, ordinary demeanour. The very picture of averageness. And yet, there's something violently remarkable about her eyes. A light that defies description. As if she can see things beyond the visible spectrum. It is simultaneously alarming and intensely attractive.

"Do you think you're insane?" I ask, resorting to professional stereotype.

"No, not now. But I have been, many times." She cocks her head backwards a little, taking a little pride in her claims.

"So, how can you tell the difference? Between sanity and insanity?" This is my last consultation of the day and I have the feeling there is some fun to be had giving this woman enough rope to play with.

"That's an easy question to answer. When I'm insane, I don't know who I am."

"And who are you now?" I lean forward a little. Sometimes these simple questions can be the most revealing.

"Let's say… Simone. Not my real name of course."

"Can you tell me your real name, Simone?" I enjoy test driving her name and I can tell she enjoys hearing it for the first time, like an actor on opening night.

"You couldn't pronounce it. Not these days. *I* can't even pronounce it these days."

I decide to set my sails fractionally against the wind. "Was there a time your name *could* be pronounced?"

"Yes. About six thousand years ago."

And there we have it. Confirmation that poor Simone is in need of help. Six thousand years probably means something to do with the Egyptians. Probably with regal connections. Why is it always the Egyptians? Or the Druids? Or the Inuits? Plain, old-fashioned, wish fulfilment. A lost mind trying to find a glamorous home. Anyway, once more unto the breach…

"If you don't mind me asking, how old are you, Simone?"

"Well, I was thirty-four when it happened, so that makes me about six-thousand-and-thirty-four, give or take." A wry smile spreads slowly across her lips. Is that a joke within a joke? Is she toying with me? What exactly seems to be the problem?

"You appreciate that would make you the oldest living human being on the planet, by a considerable margin?"

"I haven't thought of myself as a human being in quite some time, Doctor Ross."

"When was the last time you thought of yourself as human?"

"Now, there's a story," she sighs.

I glance at my Rolex. "We have plenty of time."

She laughs at this. More of a snort, in fact. I light a cigarette and pass the pack across the table. She places one in her mouth and waits for me to light it, cupping a hand around my silver-plated lighter as I lean across. Our eyes meet briefly and something is silently said.

"I get a chance to do this roughly once every two hundred

years, you know. Tell my story. The whole shebang. Warts and all. The last time was in Vienna, as I recall."

"And what were you doing in Vienna?"

"Trying to kill myself, probably."

We both acknowledge the dark honesty in this statement. The flippancy masks an undercurrent of black hopelessness.

"Would you like to tell your story now? Warts and all?"

She is unsmiling, demure. "Yes, I think that would help. Warts and all."

I sit back in my chair and wave my cigarette in an open gesture, giving her permission to take the stage, in her own time.

"Well, I was born many years ago in a province of what is now referred to as the Middle East. I was a physician in a royal household. Not the lead physician, but part of a clinical team, I suppose. And, unlike today, in those civilised times, it was not a problem for a woman to hold a position as a senior medic."

This comment makes me feel a smidgen uncomfortable. A hot tingling around my collar. I imagine that was the intention.

"My sole duty, *our* sole duty, was to create an elixir for his royal highness the pharaoh. A magic potion that would make him immortal. He was supposed to be immortal already but everyone knew – deep down – that was pure bunkum. Our job was to turn the impossible into reality. And, much more by accident than by design, I succeeded. But due to a series of events that were outside of my control, only myself and a cat were blessed with immortality."

I find myself being drawn into the narrative. She is a compelling storyteller. I genuinely want to know what happens next. Which, to be honest, is quite a novelty in my patient sessions. This could be, dare I say it, profitable.

"So what happened to the pharaoh?" I ask.

"He was poisoned, accidentally. By me. You see the

elixir I created was quite a volatile botanical mixture, distilled from a very specific list of natural ingredients and one highly unnatural ingredient."

She stirs her hand in the air above an imaginary cauldron. I note that there are none of the telltale signs that people make when they are delivering fabrications. On the contrary, her body language indicates she is recollecting a true and vivid memory.

"A comet passed through the sky when I was about thirty. Of course, in those days, no one had the foggiest idea what it was. We all assumed it was a chariot of the gods or some such mumbo-jumbo. An 'ill star' – a *disastro.* A few months later there was the most extraordinary meteor shower the world has ever seen – like a firework display." Her eyes sparkle as she looks upwards. "One fragment of the comet's tail fell to earth in the desert and, as one of the royal physicians, I had the honour of inspecting it first."

I start to put the pieces of the puzzle together, seeing my conclusions assemble in my mind's eye.

"May I guess that you were able to extract a very unique element from this lump of space rock, in a limited quantity that, once used, could never be replaced?" I sit with my pen poised above my notepad.

"That is correct, Doctor," she smiles, foxily.

"So, how was it that you, and not the pharaoh, ended up reaping the benefits of the elixir?" This tack could provide some interesting insights into any conflicts within the superego. That was the broad plan, anyway.

"Well, firstly, I tested the elixir on a cat. That creature simply could not be killed no matter how hard I tried. Ninety-nine lives and counting. So, I told the lead physician who told the pharaoh. He thought it was some cheap conjuring trick. So, he insisted that *I* take the elixir and then proceeded to have me killed in a multitude of ways. A rather bothersome business. Finally, after about a month, the pharaoh took the elixir himself and dropped dead instantly."

I wait for her to carry on, but she is hesitant to proceed, as if she has become aware of how ludicrous the story sounds. She brushes a stray hair away from her face and tips her head back a little, defiantly.

"Do you mind if we change the topic for a moment?" I suggest. After a pause, she nods. As if something has melted a little inside of her. I put down my notebook and take off my spectacles. Sometimes these simple little gestures can pay unexpected dividends.

"About four years ago, you were admitted to a psychiatric hospital about twenty miles from here. You were in a semi-catatonic state, floating in and out of consciousness. No one knew who you were or where you had come from. You simply arrived one day at the hospital."

"I'm aware of all this, but I have no specific memory of it," she states, calmly. After a moment, it's apparent she's not going to say anything further, so I continue.

"About a month ago, you suddenly and without warning regained full consciousness and were moved to this secure unit. It's my job to assess your wellbeing before we decide on… on a suitable course of action that will best meet your personal welfare requirements."

"And what are your findings so far?" she says, with the faintest hint of a smile.

I sit back a little and interlock my fingers.

"I'd like to hear a little more of your story if I may. It's helping me to build a more complete picture of who you are. What happened after the pharaoh died?"

"Well, it was impossible for me to remain in the world."

She taps cigarette ash into the little tin foil tray on the

table. "I was immortal, but I wasn't part of the royal bloodline. I was a paradox, an embarrassment. They couldn't kill me, so I was banished to the ends of the earth."

"What did that entail?" This was getting better by the minute. It would make for entertaining conversation over cocktails at James and Isobel's dinner tomorrow night. Maybe even a research paper. A seminar tour. Television interviews. A book. Film rights. The story already felt like a book. Add some smart insights and analysis and this could be a bestseller.

"It entailed a very long and very unpleasant sea journey to what is now known as Islay, an island on the west coast of Scotland. I was tossed ashore and left to fend for myself with the native community."

"And how did that work out for you?"

"Well, surprisingly quickly, I became a kind of chieftain."

I write the words 'narcissistic tendency' discreetly on my notepad.

"My immortality and my knowledge of medicine gave me a divine status on the island. I couldn't be killed, I didn't age, and I could help my fellow islanders to avoid illness – some of the time. It was idyllic, in its own simple way. But then I messed it all up."

"How so?" I recross my legs. I feel as if we were about to reach some kind of insight. A pivot.

"I fell in love." She looks at me with eyes that express a universal truth. I feel an unexpected wave of sympathy.

"Doctor," she goes on, deliberately, "to watch the person you love grow old and be ravaged by time and illness is utterly, helplessly, hopelessly painful. But to do so while you remain unchanged is horrific. Unnatural. Unrelentingly cruel. To see your offspring suffer the same fate is indescribable. In my lifetime, I've had many children, but it never gets any easier to see them age, like some time-lapse film – to turn from saplings into hollow husks before your eyes."

Again, the unexpected sympathy.

"How did you cope, with the sorrow?"

"I bloody well fought against it. With science and reason. I had created an elixir of immortality, so why not an antidote? I spent many hundreds of years trying to distil my salvation on that island, but nothing worked. The extra-terrestrial ingredient was missing, and all that I could come up with was a potent, intoxicating ether, which the islanders named *uisige beatha*."

I smile a conspiratorial smile. It was a twist that brought a little warmth to my normally chilly heart.

"Of course," I say, "*uisge beatha* – whisky – the 'water of life'. I heard an interesting legend once about Scotch whisky."

"Really?" she asks, one eyebrow raised.

"If you drink just the right amount of whisky every day, they say you'll live forever."

She barks a sudden, short laugh. "Well there's an element of truth to that. But unfortunately not the right element."

"So, did you remain on the island after that?"

"No. My idyll began to feel like a prison with too many painful memories. So I began my wanderings."

"Where did you travel to?"

"Everywhere."

"Really?"

"When you have an infinite amount of time, the world becomes a very small place indeed."

She begins to ramble a little. There is mention of Morocco and Persia, Bombay and Shanghai, palaces and military campaigns. To be honest, many of the terms and names she uses are unintelligible. Pronounced with heavy accents and strung together in unusual ways. She senses that I'm becoming distracted and so she truncates her travels, making an expression not unlike that used when one realises one is explaining something to a small child who is never going to grasp the true meaning of what is being explained.

"I spent most of World War Two in Norway because a high-ranking Nazi became aware of my condition. The infamous Telemark heavy water research was only partly to do with developing atomic weapons, you know. The real aim was to develop an elixir that could create an Aryan army of not-quite-immortals, but super-mortals. The Thousand Year Reich. It was a blessing that the Allies managed to bravely scupper the plans before they got too far. And, of course, I escaped with my life. As usual."

I decide to set off the beaten track of logic and set foot gingerly in the softer ground of emotion.

"How does your condition make you feel?"

She relaxes noticeably, and a wistful expression passes across her face.

"George Bernard Shaw suggested that every exiled person fantasises about returning to a perfect version of their home that never really existed. And no matter how hard they try, they will never feel truly at home in their new surroundings. That, kind sir, is exactly how I feel."

I sit back and allow her to expand. Her speech is languid, like the air in the room.

"I've spent a lot of time working in museums and schools, teaching history. Or, rather, teaching the version of history that happens to be currently in vogue. Written by the victors, and all that. Any time I get into a tight spot, I simply have to wait a few decades for the status quo to change. For the revolution to happen. For the uprising to rise up. And, when it does, it's easy to simply get lost and disappear in the chaos. I just slip through the cracks of time."

She holds up a hand and rubs her first two fingers and

thumb together, scattering imaginary sand into dust, blowing it away with a puff of air. The air causes some actual dust to sleepily circulate in a beam of late afternoon sunlight. There's something deeply magnetic about the timbre of her voice, the syrupy shine in those eyes.

"You move on once every thirty years or so. Outlive those you get close to. Or just pop out for a pint of milk and disappear into the night. No one really exists for more than a generation or two after they die. Even those individuals who make it into the history books are only avatars and amalgams – endlessly reinterpreted and redefined by each passing generation. I've worked in finance and accumulated and squandered vast wealth. I've been philanthropic and utterly wasteful. I've had self-destructive spells that lasted centuries and resulted in no self-destruction. I've been cruel and I've been penitent. I've spent as many years in every kind of jail as I have working for every kind of church. I've experienced the highest levels of zen calm by meditating for years on end. I've been a reckless playgirl without morals, and I've also been one of the single greatest forces for good in the field of medicine – arguably the greatest doctor that ever lived. I've seen the full spectrum of life's colours at every wavelength. And it's brought me to this point in time, here, now, with you."

Momentarily, I feel as if something has shifted slightly in the room. Nothing to be concerned about, but I feel as if my motivation for being here has changed imperceptibly. Gravity has been diluted. I blink and things appear to return to normal, although normal now veers slightly towards a different locus.

"Every few centuries, it takes its toll. The brain of *homo sapiens* is not designed to be engulfed by the sheer volume of years and, eventually, I go a little cuckoo. Or a lot cuckoo, to be frank. Nothing that a few years in a vegetative state doesn't seem to fix, though. And then here I am again. Right as rain."

Tiny swirling specks of matter caught in sunlight appear to gradually slow down and then come to a standstill. They sparkle like the atoms of a rainbow. Everything in the room is frozen. I look directly into her eyes and find that I am unable to look away. Not that I would want to. I have never been quite so comfortable and relaxed as this. This is exactly where I want to be. Such beautiful eyes. She continues talking, softly.

"Over the years, I've picked up a few tricks that allow me to temper the pace and tone of my speech, and paint an illusion that's hard to resist. So why resist, Doctor Ross? Release all that tension and fall back, back into yourself, your true self, release all the pressure, find the younger version of yourself, the innocent, the idealist, the child, no cares or worries, let them all go."

I inhale a deep breath that makes me shudder slightly, unexpectedly emotional, heavy eyes glassy with teardrops.

"There, there, Doctor Ross. That's a good fellow. In a moment, we'll get up and leave this room and then leave the building together, through the security doors, and then we'll get into your car, and we'll drive away from this place. Then you'll drop me off at the nearest town and carry on with your day as usual. In a few weeks, you'll receive some anonymous financial compensation for your troubles, more than enough to cover any disruption to your career caused by my disappearance. So you can relax now, everything is taken care of. Now, do you have any questions before we leave?"

I search my mind for a long and short time, trying to catch up with my thoughts.

"Your story, is it all true?" I ask. My voice sounds like its being spoken by someone else, a child perhaps, and yet it is unmistakably my voice.

"It's as true as the sun rising into the sky tomorrow morning. Which, as we all know, is nothing but an illusion caused by the rotation of the earth. And is, by no means, a certainty. Even the image we see of the sun is an atmospheric mirage, and one that is eight minutes old. It's all smoke and mirrors, Doctor. A magician's trick. There is no such thing as truth, only perception. My story can be perceived in any way you like. But, from my point of view, I can assure you that every single word is accurate."

Slowly, she stands up and holds out a hand for me to take, smiling, like a mother to a small child.

"Now, shall we go? Please allow me to help you with your jacket and keys, Doctor. That's it. Take your time, no rush. We've all the time in the world."

The Vessel

On the day after my thirtieth birthday, just after lunch, I decided to end my life.

For a while, I had been considering the question of when would be the best time of year to die. I'd always liked that period when late summer gradually blended with early autumn. The change in the sunlight and the charge of seasonal anticipation in the air as the heat started to fade. But dying at one's favourite time of year might be harder to endure. Leaving behind all the beauty of nature would be painful. Perhaps a miserable, damp, cold January afternoon would be better. A despondent, *what's-the-point-in-carrying-on?* kind of day. A day where death would seem like an opportunity. An adventure.

In the end, I decided to end my life in early November on a mild day with a blank grey sky. I had spent the morning tidying up some final bits of paperwork, and there was a neat pile of Manila envelopes arranged on the kitchenette table. I'd prepared a light lunch of porridge and honey (technically a breakfast rather than a lunch, but what difference would it make now?), before washing the dishes carefully and putting them away. And now, I was seated in my armchair in the small sitting room of my quarters, with a cup of tea, a syringe and a length of rubber tubing on the low table in front of me. The record player was playing some Vaughn Williams quietly. I felt empty and somehow heavy at the same time, a lead weight hanging in my chest. I sighed, sat back, closed my eyes, and considered the life I had lived.

My early, fuzzy memories were happy ones. Smiling parents doting over their only child, the centre of their universe. A windy day at the beach, with a kite. Feeding a horse. The excitement of taking a train to London. And then, abruptly, my parents disappeared from the narrative completely. For years, even after I fully realised the nature of their deaths, I kept thinking they would return. A meal at a country restaurant to celebrate my mother's birthday. A shared bottle of wine and a brandy *digestif.* A patch of ice on a dark country road. A corner taken too fast in a new motor car. And that was that.

I was taken in by my mother's mother. One of the first of many confusing rules was that I was never to refer to her as my grandmother and instead was to call her Aunt Edith. She was a cold, austere woman with Victorian values and a porcelain heart. I moved in to her house in a small market town and tried to regain something of my happy demeanour, but it was a losing battle. There were no more trips to the beach or to colourful toy shops. Instead, there was regimental order revolving around school, household chores, church and Aunt Edith's small circle of female cronies. At school, I found it hard to make friends. Looking back, I think this was because I didn't want to get too close to anyone in case that closeness was suddenly ripped away. I immersed myself in my studies and found I had a natural aptitude for the sciences. And so, for most of my childhood and adolescence, my true friends were the books on the shelf of my bedroom written by long-dead scientists.

When I was seventeen, I was sent away for a week to a sort of boot camp for gifted children, despite my protestations that I really did not want to go. The scientific challenges were enjoyable enough. But the social aspect of the camp was tortuous. I spent the entire week trying to find ways to hide from the others, my nose usually stuffed inside a book, blushing furiously when anyone tried to make conversation. I couldn't wait to get back to the relative normality of Aunt Edith's house and the sanctuary of my bedroom study. Feeling depressed on my own was always more bearable than feeling depressed in the company of others.

A week after my return, Aunt Edith received a phone call from the school requesting that she and I meet with the headmaster as soon as possible. It transpired that the organisers of the camp had seen some very special qualities in me and I had been selected to be a member of the first cohort of students to attend a highly exclusive further education establishment that was opening at the beginning of the new academic year. All my fees would be paid by the government, I would be lodged at comfortable new halls of residence with 'all mod cons' and I would be excused from National Service. It was one of the few times I saw Aunt Edith show anything close to emotion – a strange mix of pride and resentment. Before I had a chance to gather myself, she told the headmaster I would be delighted to accept the offer.

Three months later, I had moved in to my new accommodation at the Charteris Academy, hidden in the wooded heart of rural England. The campus was built in the modern European style, all concrete geometry and brutal right angles. It looked vaguely like the photographs I'd seen of wartime gun emplacements in Northern France, with long horizontal slit windows and a complete absence of decoration. Somehow, it suited my temperament and my attitude to work. On the first day of term, the students were greeted by Professor Carmichael, who had hosted the previous summer's camp. After a brief welcome presentation in the main lecture theatre, Carmichael explained that – as a formality – we would all have to sign the Official Secrets Act, given that some of the research carried out at Charteris may have military applications and we couldn't allow this valuable information to fall into enemy hands. Some of the students in the auditorium seemed a little taken aback, but I found it exhilarating. At last, my mental capacities could be put to good use, helping to safeguard the lives of my fellow countrymen. Signing the paperwork, I felt an unprecedented sense of self-confidence, albeit cushioned by the underlying feeling of grey emptiness that always seemed to dog me.

Life at Charteris quickly fell into an easy routine. Up early most days to run a few miles around the campus. A simple breakfast of tea, porridge and honey. Lecture and tutorial discussion groups until lunchtime. Applied study, as it was called, after lunch. This involved a mix of textbook-based reading, watching scientific films and, mostly, lab work. Many of the films and books were marked 'classified' and contained a variety of novel theoretical ideas and data gathered from all around the world. Although the ultimate purpose of my studies remained cloudy, I could glimpse here and there that I was helping to develop weaponry of an entirely new kind – tailoring biological and chemical agents in ways to inflict maximum damage on the populations of potential adversaries. None of this filled me with any sense of guilt. But neither did it fill me with any true sense of fulfilment. My main motivation was simply to complete the tasks that landed on my desk, taking each day as it came.

The months turned into years. It became vaguely apparent that Charteris was not like other institutions with formal timetabling for the completion of courses. There was more a general sense that both students and tutors were working together towards a flexible set of objectives. The idea of a formal qualification was never mentioned, partly because the curriculum changed rapidly and regularly to meet the changing needs of the department heads whom, we assumed, were being briefed by the military and the government. It was curious to think that, many miles away, agents in foreign espionage were risking their lives to determine the course of our research here within the security of our brushed concrete walls. These ideas were never discussed openly, which made them all the more curious.

There was a social life of sorts on the campus. Our spacious canteen could be easily transformed into a cinema, a bar, a dancehall and even a theatre. Although, to be honest, I had little interest in these trivial distractions. I found my colleagues' preoccupations with sports, entertainment and romance to be tiresome. For this reason, I often chose to continue my studies well into the evenings and, over the course of a few years, I became aware that the 'powers that be' had singled me out as a high achiever – both in terms of my technical abilities but also as someone who could be relied upon to get things done, someone with a sense of focus. I sometimes wondered what it would be like to be with a woman, and of course had the physical urges that every young man experiences. But my awkwardness made it impossible for me to strike up even the simplest of conversations with a member of the opposite sex. I suspected this may have become one of the reasons for my rapid ascension to group head and then department head by the time I was just twenty-seven years old.

At this age, I had hardened my personality somewhat. I had targets to achieve and deadlines to meet and I found that the best way to motivate my subordinates was through simply being myself – cold, aloof, driven, logical. This also resulted in my department attaining a higher rate of breakthrough than others, from which I took some minor satisfaction.

A curious thing happened in my second year as

department head, when I was supervising a lab experiment. A young student named Page was entering the secure lab area through its 'airlock' system, dressed in the protective rubber suit, gloves and boots that were required to isolate the wearer from noxious materials. About ten seconds before he entered the airlock, I noticed a tiny gap in the zipper that held the back of the hood to the neck of the garment. Two teeth in the zipper had come loose meaning that the suit appeared to be fastened securely, but there was in fact a minuscule gap that would expose Page to the atmosphere within the lab. I should have called out to stop him entering the airlock, but found myself unable to utter a word. Within a minute or so, Page had suffered a sudden and fatal reaction to the very toxin he had helped to develop, the cells of his body raging against him and eventually reducing his organs to a kind of soup. As the emergency klaxons rang out, I felt strangely disconnected from my part in his demise.

And now, here I was, preparing to end my own life. I looked down at the syringe. This wasn't the first time I had prepared to commit suicide. There had been several attempts in recent months that had, disappointingly, led to nothing. My problem was not related to any queasiness regarding the process of entering oblivion. It was more to do with not wanting to miss out on the future. The approaching decades would see great leaps in the fields of space exploration, quantum physics, computing, robotics and medicine – marvels that would leave me breathless. But the years would also be filled with the terrible gnawing emptiness that I simply could not shake. Every moment of every day was becoming a struggle, maintaining a mask of professional contentment when, inside, I was a hollow man. An empty vessel. I decided to take a walk in the campus grounds to organise my thoughts.

I headed towards my favourite place for reflection, a

secluded square of grass with a few young birch trees and a couple of benches, surrounded on all sides by the blank low walls of the institution buildings. Taking a seat, I felt the weight of my existence clinging darkly in my chest. I lit a cigarette, looking up at the low grey clouds that blanketed the sky.

I became aware of the sound of footsteps on gravel and looked to my right to see the figure of a short, stocky middle-aged man in a boiler suit approaching.

"Mind if I join you?"

The man gently waved the Thermos flask he held in his right hand and smiled warmly. I would have preferred solitude, but I shuffled along the bench a little to provide enough space for the man to sit down.

He proceeded to pour steaming tea into the cup of the flask and held it out for me to take. At first, I raised a hand to politely decline the offer, but the man smiled and placed the cup in my hand.

"It has a little extra fortification, to keep the cold at bay. A 'special compound' from a distillery in the Hebrides."

I smiled back at him and took a sip of the tea. There was a very subtle hint of something medicinal in the taste, but it was not unpleasant.

We sat together in silence for a while, watching a small bird hopping around the grass pecking at the ground.

"We've been keeping an eye on you for a while, Charles."

I turned to look at the man, but he kept his face forward. His hair was thinning, but was groomed immaculately – combed and pomaded in fine lines back from his temples, shaved precisely behind the ears and on his neck. His tortoiseshell spectacles looked expensive and I noticed a faint scent of cologne. All these details were at odds with his boiler suit and heavy work boots. At first, I had assumed that the man was a technician or maybe even a groundskeeper. But his accent betrayed a public school education at the very least.

"We know you've been having a bit of a rough time of it and… considering some changes."

He turned his head to look at me, still smiling, as I nervously finished off the tea.

"But there is so much more you can do for Charteris and there is so much more we can do for you. We have a new programme in the pipeline that is truly groundbreaking – streets ahead of anything we've ever achieved before – bringing together the very latest in bio-mechanicals, engineering, atomics…"

He peered at me over his glasses with genuine pride in his eyes. "We want you to be at the very centre of this programme. You will make history, my boy."

I was about to say something when I realised that my mouth felt curiously numb. I tried to raise my hand to my lips, but my arm wouldn't respond. A second later, my head slumped forward onto my chest and I began to tilt to the left. The man put his arm around my shoulder to stop me from falling to the ground, but he appeared to be completely unsurprised and unconcerned by my condition. As my head lolled onto his shoulder, and my consciousness began to drift away, I was able to see the man's face in profile, disappearing away from me down the tunnel of my darkening vision. He quietly repeated his previous phrase, but was looking to the distance rather than toward me.

"Yes, you will make history, my boy."

*

I was standing in the secure laboratory, handling a test tube filled with a new ultra-toxin in liquid form. It didn't occur to me that I had ever worn a safety suit in the past, because I didn't need to wear one now. As far as I was concerned, I had always been able to handle toxins of any form without putting myself at risk.

I looked down at the sleek metallic plates that covered my forearm, held in place by their tiny rivets. The green military paint was scuffed here and there and each plate had its individual serial number stencilled in small utilitarian numerals at one corner. My wrist joint was covered with a black rubber sheath, corrugated in order to provide flexibility. My elegant hand was engineered to perfection – a combination of tiny metal rods with pneumatic controllers, gracefully curved plates, rubber fingertips and palm pads. The mechanical musculature in my hand had a grip that could crush a billiard ball, but the care with which I held the test tube between index finger and thumb had been calculated to a microscopic tolerance.

I focussed briefly on my reflection in the safety glass of the lab, to check for compromises. Steel skull plates painted matt green, with some mild abrasions. Two adjustable Leica lenses for eyes, focussing light onto my optical processing matrix, sending data to the intricacies of my logic gateway, connecting to the organic parts of my brain, held in their titanium capsules, completely sealed off from the outside world.

I felt nothing as I went about my lab work. The closest I came to any emotion was the intangible sense of duty I had towards carrying out my orders, something not unlike pride, but watered down to one part in a thousand. I worked all day and all though the night, as I had no requirement for sleeping or eating. The marvel that is the tiny atomic motor located behind my sternum plate would operate tirelessly for a millennium. And my ability to self-diagnose meant I could perform running repairs on every aspect of my body, giving me a virtually infinite lifespan. My unique organic components allowed me to problem-solve in ways that no other machine could. So, not only was I a virtually invincible lab technician, I was also a professor of science – constantly accumulating and applying knowledge in ways that, until now, were impossible.

Upon exiting the lab and undergoing my disinfection regime, I retired to my workshop quarters to make a subtle improvement to the artificial muscles located within my lower back. Removing my skull, I placed it on the bench behind me, dislocating my arms from their metal sockets and rotating them through half a revolution to make it easier to remove the metal plates above my hips. An hour later, I had enhanced my ability to run and jump by a factor of point zero one percent. I was already the fastest individual on the campus, but my logic gateway was programmed to always seek improvement when possible. As I strode through the corridors of the facility, my human colleagues either ignored me or looked upon me with a sense of uneasy awe. Although I was programmed to recognise these facial expressions, and react accordingly, they were meaningless to me in terms of their emotional currency.

I suspected there was another one, like me, at another facility in a different part of the country. I overheard a telephone conversation between the Programme Coordinator and his superior. It was as if he had forgotten I was in the room. Sometimes I think he mistakes me for a machine. Remembering my presence, he ushered me out into the corridor.

There are three things I have noticed about the Programme Coordinator. He always wears a boiler suit. He always wears the same cologne. And, in many of his reports, he mentions that his work programme is centred around the novel combination of mechanical engineering with primate cortexes, but he has never once defined the species of primate to which he is referring.

The incident occurred late one evening as I stood in a dark

corner of the empty lab performing my nightly internal diagnostic checks. This process involved a requirement for me to power down all non-essential systems and, I suppose, to any passer-by I appeared completely inert. A technician called Porter entered the lab shortly after three and quietly made his way to the main store whereby he used a small torch to locate a vial filled with a supertoxin of the omega strain, which he proceeded to place in the breast pocket of his lab coat. He removed an identical vial and replaced it carefully in the store before turning to exit the lab.

In less than a second, my logic cortex had fully rebooted and performed several thousand calculations. There appeared to be a very high probability that Porter was attempting to steal the supertoxin, and a comparably high probability that his intention was to offer the sample to one of our nation's enemies, perhaps in return for money or status. If the compound fell into enemy hands, this would put Charteris at risk. And the Coordinator had programmed me to protect Charteris and its staff *at all costs*. In fact, it was my prime directive. Porter's actions meant he could no longer be considered a staff member and therefore I was compelled to use decisive autonomous force to prevent him from carrying out his mission. Bending my knees slightly, I was able to leap across the lab in a single bound, the rubberised soles of my feet gaining purchase just a few inches away from where Porter stood. As he turned to face me, a look of shocked surprise on his face, I extended my arm as forcefully as possible, ramming my palm into his nose, disintegrating his features and sending his spectacles far into the grey matter of his brain. His body immediately went limp and, as he slowly toppled backwards, I carefully extracted the toxin from his pocket. When he hit the lab floor, a myriad vectors of blood ejected from his broken skull, covering the floor with an abstract explosion of colour.

In the milliseconds that followed, I evaluated the situation. Porter, who had been a member of the Charteris staff, had revealed himself to be an enemy agent. Therefore, any other member of staff could also be an enemy agent – even the Coordinator. The only way to protect Charteris – *at all costs* – was to recognise this fact and act upon it: all members of staff and, in fact, all people, had the potential to destroy Charteris. The only person I knew with absolute certainty not to be an enemy agent was myself. And so, logically, I resolved to become the true custodian of Charteris by crushing the vial in my hand. Sixty-seven days later, the lack of radio and television transmissions meant I could safely assume every human being on the planet was dead and the threat to Charteris had been successfully neutralised.

*

Over the next few months I began cleaning and tidying the campus. After loading the corpses on to the back of a lorry and dumping them a few miles away on farmland, I returned to the facility and methodically cleaned and secured every room. Many of the administrative and recreational rooms were of no use to me, so I locked them up for good. The same applied to the toxin labs, although I did decide to keep one chemical research wing fully maintained. The small atomic power generator continued to run at optimum power and the engineering hub, where I spent most of my time, became my main home.

I fell into a self-imposed routine: checking the security of the base, performing research in order to upgrade my performance, maintaining and enhancing my mind and body, self-diagnostic checks, a daily sweep for radio transmissions. The empty static, devoid of humanity, always gave me a sense of what could be loosely described as satisfaction.

As time progressed, I started to become aware of more and more sensations that I assumed to be akin to emotion. When I made the decision to strip all the dull green paint from my body and replace it with a perfect chromium finish, I felt 'pride'. When I took to listening to gramophone recordings of Bach, I felt a precursor of 'wonder' filter through my cortex. And, on those nights when my diagnostic check revealed a temporarily depressed level of performance, I began to classify this as 'loneliness'.

I also started to perform a kind of meditation in the hours just before dawn. I would walk to the highest part of the facility, the roof terrace above the Coordinator's quarters, and stand gazing out at the distant horizon, beyond the security gates, beyond the surrounding woodland, beyond the empty farms and houses, watching the colour of the sky transform through its ritual spectrum as the sun rose. At first, it was a good way to test my visual acuity and light sensitivity. But, after a while, it became something that affected my higher brain functions in ways that were hard to describe. A contemplative feeling of being part of something much greater than myself. Something that went far beyond my understanding and even the understanding of the men who created me.

I began to wonder if it would be possible to integrate these new emotions into my being. Like an upgrade. Would they be a benefit or a drawback? As a thin line of blue light began to spread across the horizon, I thought of something that the Coordinator once said in passing about a machine that dreamt he was a man being the same as a man who dreamt he was a machine. The statement always gave my logic gateway an uncomfortably warm ache.

Shutting the apertures of my ocular lenses for a moment, I tried to clear my thoughts. Locked away, in a corner of my head, there was a fleeting memory of a young man who tried to take his own life on the day after his thirtieth birthday. A highly intelligent young man who had been suffering from paranoia, anxiety and depression for a long time. It was a suicide attempt that was unsuccessful, but left him severely incapacitated. Trapped within himself. Rattling around inside a vessel of unnatural design. But a design that was entirely feasible within the comprehension of the young man's brain. A brain that was, to the outside world, in a vegetative state – being kept alive by a machine. A brain being kept alive by a mother's mother who simply could not bring herself to let go of her child's child by signing the appropriate consent forms. A brain within the broken body of a man who would see out his days bedridden in a medical facility somewhere in the wooded heart of England. But the recollection was momentary – the tiniest fraction of a millisecond – and was easily erased.

Far away, the distant sound of a jet engine broke the silence. I opened my lenses to scan the horizon, and saw the graceful curve of an aircraft slice through the sky, a bullet of silver shining in the dawn twilight. I adopted a defensive pose and unholstered the sidearm at my hip. Within moments the craft had crossed the landscape and slowed to a halt, hovering just above the security gates, its twin jets deafening. I focussed my lenses to maximum magnification and saw that it was not quite an aircraft, but rather a humanoid machine – like me – with aeroplane wings attached to its shoulder blades. Its waspish waist and slender legs gave it an unmistakably female form.

It crossed the final yards of airspace before gently descending onto the roof terrace directly in front of me, the noise of the engines gradually powering down, the wingtip lights pulsing, a spectacular silhouette.

And as the sun finally breached the horizon, she turned her head towards me, eye lenses ablaze. The atomic motor in my chest seemed to burn with an intensity that matched the power of the sun. This was a new day. This was a new day like no other. Today, I felt glad to be alive.

The Witness

I arrive, once again, at a place I have never been before. As the taxi pulls away, I put down my suitcase and take in the view. A sandy cove surrounded by impressive, rocky cliffs. Turquoise waters sparkling. A little settlement of whitewashed buildings clinging to the hillside. A gentle paradise.

Picking up my case, I make my way down a flight of steep stone steps and into the siesta-quiet village. Shutters are closed. Shops are locked. A dog lies sleeping in the shade. Nearing the beach, a small café with red and white gingham tablecloths comes into view.

A man in his fifties is sitting at a table, sipping an espresso. I take a seat nearby. The waiter brings a glass of water before retreating behind the bar. Cicada. Seabirds. Waves lapping at the shore.

"You're wondering where you are, Mr Thomas," states the espresso drinker, flatly. "And you're wondering who I am. But you already know the answers to these questions."

We watch a gull cross the bay, swooping down to the water to ambush an unseen fish.

"So... where am I, and who are you?" I ask, tentatively.

The man turns to face me and there is a moment of recognition. I know those intelligent, genial eyes.

"We are in a small village on the northern coast of Majorca, and my name is Lawrence Hastings. I taught English at your grammar school. But none of this really matters. There is no matter, no substance to these details. Quite literally."

I become aware that I feel very isolated from my surroundings.

"Your mind is elsewhere, Mr Thomas. Time is against you, and there is something you need to do. I'm here to assist in that process, but please remember all this is simply a conjurer's trick. Very vivid, very detailed – but a conjurer's trick nonetheless."

A sea breeze catches the edge of the paper napkin beneath my glass.

"Look at this." Hastings picks up a white ceramic ashtray emblazoned with the red and black crest of a local *cerveza*. "Accurate in every detail. Colour. Shape. Size. Weight. This is not an amalgam. For our purposes, it's the real thing. The human mind has the capacity to store memory in truly amazing detail – even the ephemera of life. My spectacles, for example. Here they are, recreated in glorious detail like cherished artefacts in a museum."

Hastings chuckles as he cleans his eyeglasses with a handkerchief, before replacing them on his nose. The sun disappears briefly behind a hazy cloud, shadows momentarily losing definition.

"I've been dead for some time, Mr Thomas, but you know that already. Yet, here I am in technicolour, enjoying one of my final performances. As our Mexican cousins would have us believe, we all live on after death in the minds of the people we make an impression on, until the memories eventually fade and we dissolve into the collective consciousness – eternally present and yet not really present at all."

Hastings gives a contented sigh, places some coins on the table and stands to go. "You'll figure it all out soon enough, Mr Thomas. I'll be around if you need anything." He walks off in the direction of the cliffs, barefoot, leaving prints in the white sand.

The waiter provides me with the key to a small room above the café. I unpack the contents of my bag – simple toiletries, lightweight clothes, a few books, an empty photograph frame – and take a seat on a little wicker chair to enjoy the early evening air from the tiny balcony.

The cliffs have turned an impossible peach colour, and appear to float slightly above the milky blue horizon. A couple walk hand-in-hand along the edge of the water while dreamlike flamenco guitar notes drift up from a gramophone in the café. A dog barks in the distance.

Calmly, I wonder if I am dead. As strange as the day's events have been, I am surrounded by a pleasant familiarity that offers a wealth of comfort. I would try to remember more about who I am and how I got here, but the part of my mind responsible for asking these questions has long gone.

As I close the window, I see my reflection in the glass – a clean-shaven man in his thirties with a neat haircut, dressed in a light suit, shirt open at the collar. Moving closer, I look for clues in the grey eyes that stare back. I find only my own questioning gaze.

As I leave the room to go downstairs for dinner I hear the sound of a train in the distance, faint but somehow determined.

Hastings is sitting at a table in the café, a napkin stuffed into his collar. "Take a seat, Mr Thomas," he says, topping up his glass of red wine. The waiter brings me some bread, soup and a glass of water, while Hastings grazes over three dishes of *tapas*.

"Any the wiser?" asks Hastings between mouthfuls of *chorizo*. My silence prompts him to finish eating, dab his lips with his napkin and settle back in his chair. As the sun sets, the waiter lights a candle on the table. Its light flickers in Hastings' spectacles.

"Some things are a little too hard for the mind to

comprehend, dear boy, especially when it's attempting to comprehend itself. It plays tricks to get the job done. Invents characters and situations to preserve some kind of decorum. Or, in your case, to reach some kind of equilibrium. Tomorrow, you will have to make a small journey. Follow the coastal path. When you arrive at your destination, things will become clearer. Get some rest, Mr Thomas. *Buenas noches*."

After Hastings makes his departure, I finish my soup and retire to my room. Lying on the bed, I hear the distant sound of the surf on the shore coming and going, coming and going. I absent-mindedly watch the beam from a lighthouse make sweeping shapes on the ceiling at curiously irregular intervals. An absent mind creating mathematical puzzles. I drift into sleep, but it's hard to tell where reality ends and dreams begin.

A parallelogram of sunlight on the wooden floorboards. Sounds of activity in the street below. Deliveries. Boats. Gulls. Lively conversation in Spanish. Within half an hour, I'm dressed and ready for the day – a water bottle and map in my canvas shoulder bag, hiking boots tightly laced, a mariner's cap to keep the sun at bay.

Leaving the village, I follow the coastal path to a point where it snakes up into the hills behind the cliffs. I continue for about an hour, occasionally stopping to take in the view. The village is a tiny cluster of white squares far below. I reach a saddle in the landscape between two peaks and find myself in an upland valley. I follow a straight track through a deserted landscape. A buzzard circles overhead in the clear blue sky.

After a while, I spy a footbridge crossing a railway line in the distance, curiously out of place in the dusty landscape. From a hundred yards away, I can see a boy on the bridge, looking down at the railway line with a set of binoculars. The air is heavy and uneasy in the afternoon heat. In the distance I hear a train. Faint but somehow determined.

I approach cautiously and watch the boy take a notebook from his satchel and write something down before putting the binoculars back to his eyes. Engrossed. Tenacious. Obsessive. Dedicated. At first he doesn't hear the two other boys approaching. But, as they clatteringly dismount their bicycles, he automatically takes a step back, flattening his back to the railings of the bridge. The train is louder now, its presence increasing.

The two boys move in on their prey, circling. A ritual, animal dance, passed down the generations by those naturally selected to hunt for weakness in others. A notebook snatched and thrown over the bridge. Spectacles knocked to the ground. A punch to the stomach.

From my vantage point, I only catch elements of the verbal assault, delivered in English. References to a failed suicide attempt. Nut job. Spastic. Retard. The train is much closer now, unrelenting in its approach.

The two grab a leg each and an unspoken line is crossed. The boy is manhandled awkwardly over the railings and dangled upside down over his fate. The train arrives, invisible beneath the bridge, but dominating the scene with its scream – reducing the other characters to frantic mime actors.

My heart is racing but I'm unable to move. The boys struggle to hold a leg each, false laughter failing to hide the fear in their faces. Gone too far. No going back. Oh fuck. One of the legs struggles to get free and kicks its captor full in the face, sending him reeling backwards. The second captor is left holding the remaining leg, now twice as heavy. The laws of physics take over. Hands struggle to retain a grip. A misjudged release. The leg falls from view. An unearthly cracking noise, just audible above the leviathan noise of the train.

The two youths look at one another in disbelief before

running to the opposite side of the bridge to peer over the railings at the train tracks. From my position, I see them stare directly downwards for an immeasurable length of time. Finally, one moves back from the railings, followed shortly later by the other. Without a word and without looking at one another they pick up their bicycles and tear away from the bridge, towards me.

The first boy cycles past me in a blur, his nose bloodied. The second skids to a stop, dismounts roughly and approaches me in a calculated way – his eyes measuring the risk posed by my proximity to the crime. The word 'witness' jumps into my mind, with innumerable connotations spreading out in all directions like poison ivy. Without hesitation the boy punches me full in the face. Not a warning, more of a statement of fact. Despite the force of the punch, I remain standing, my face numb. He is inches away from my face, breathing hard, eyes like granite.

"Not a word", he states. "Not a single fucking word to no one. Ever."

He turns, gets on his bicycle and takes off into the distance, pedalling fast, but perfectly in control.

I take a seat on a nearby wall, realising that my school uniform shirt is splattered with blood, my thirteen-year-old body is shaking. The Spanish mountain terrain has gone, replaced with the urban landscape of my childhood. Smoky red brick walls and hedges. Tarmac and kerbstones. I turn my head upwards and pinch the bridge of the nose, looking up through telegraph lines at an overcast sky. The sound of the distant train has become so quiet, it's hard to tell if it's real or imagined.

I sit for a long time in the vinyl armchair beside the bed, staring out of the window at a tree. My arthritic fingers are trembling gently, like an uncertain pianist, and I know there's something I need to do, but it's always just out of reach and no one ever listens. Things have changed so much. And all I have now are glimpses. I'm old, so very old, and I don't know where I am.

People come and go in this room, in their medical uniforms. Always busy, always smiling, and I always smile back at them. It's just what you do, I suppose. Glimpses are all I have these days. Lawrence Hastings. Nice chap. Loved cricket. It's time for my bath now. I'm so old. Skin like brown paper or an old leaf. Something I need to do. Something I need to say.

It's another day and she's here again. The pretty one who smiles that sad smile. Thinks I'm her father. Mostly I just sit in silence and look out of the window at the tree. But, today, I'm chatting away. Telling her all about Hastings and, would she believe, I saw him on a Spanish island of all places, and he hadn't aged a bit.

And then something peculiar happens. It's as if my mind re-engages its gears and, with no effort whatsoever on my part, I'm me again. I look at Rebecca, darling Becca, and say her name for the first time in an age. She looks at me with tears of surprise in her eyes.

"Dad! It's you! It's really you!"

We chat for twenty minutes over a cup of tea and, although my memory is flaky, it's definitely me again. I even remember little Phoebe's name, amazed to hear she's old enough to go to university next year. Rebecca is astonished. She says, candidly, that she'd given up hope of ever having another coherent conversation with me. It appears that I come and go, come and go. But there's much more going these days.

And then, I tell her. I tell her the secret I have been carrying around in my heart for seven decades. The secret that decomposed part of me from the inside out. Being a witness to a violent death at such a young age. And never saying a word, not a single word, to no one, ever. Kenneth Watson. That was the boy's name. The boy who didn't commit suicide although everyone thought he did. I ask Rebecca to write the name down and take it to the police. And I tell her that I couldn't say a word to anyone because it was my brother, your Uncle Christopher, who was partly responsible for Kenneth's death and wholly responsible for providing me with a lifelong burden of soul-destroying silence. But I can see in her eyes that we are losing one another again and, before I know it, she's a stranger to me. A stranger with a heartbroken face.

I arrive, once again, at a place I have never been before. As the taxi pulls away, I put down my suitcase and take in the view. A sandy cove surrounded by impressive, rocky cliffs. Turquoise waters sparkling. A little settlement of whitewashed buildings clinging to the hillside. A gentle paradise.

Leaving my suitcase by the roadside, I walk down through the village, past a familiar looking man in his fifties seated outside a café drinking an espresso. He smiles genially as I walk past but says nothing. Removing my shoes and socks, I make my way over the white sand to the water's edge. Deliberately, I take off my linen suit, shirt and finally my underwear, folding everything carefully to form a neat, square pile on the sand. I wind my wristwatch, place it alongside my wallet on top of the pile, and wade into the ocean.

It's that magical time of day when the late afternoon sun begins to carve ultramarine shadows into the rocks. The temperature of the ocean is Goldilocks perfect. I walk forward until the water is up to my chest, and then fall into a sedate breast stroke, following a course out of the bay and into the sea. The sounds of the village gradually become distant until they dissolve into nothing. I swim on and on and on, gliding through the water effortlessly, until I find I have left the land so far behind there is only ocean in every direction all the way to the horizon. I stop swimming and tread water, noticing that the waves are gradually settling until, after a while, the surface of the ocean is like a mirror reflecting the cloudless sky above.

There is no breeze, no sound. Only blue in all directions, above and below. A final series of ripples expands across the water forming perfect circles, ever-expanding but also ever-fading, until there is no movement. And as I dissolve into the blue, my fears and regrets and secrets dissolve away too. And I would feel foolish for wasting all those years, and sad for the boy and his family that I betrayed, and spite for the malevolent brother that I didn't, and regret that I was never really the person I had set out to be, but I have lost the capacity to feel anything at all.

The Ghosts

It was on the third day of the camp that she arrived in his life, breezily sitting down beside him in the canteen at lunchtime and exclaiming, "How's it going, Scotty?" He was confused. His name wasn't Scott. She pointed at his knapsack on the bench beside him, emblazoned with an embroidered patch that said 'Antarctica' under a stylised image of a penguin. He blushed a little. The bag contained his notebooks, pencils, penknife, slide rule, protractor, compasses, comb, talcum, medicine, toothbrush and toothpaste. He carried it with him at all times. Just in case. He now felt embarrassed by it. Although something about the girl's manner put him at ease. She seemed like fun, which was a novelty in his life. She had smiling eyes.

"If I'm to be Captain R.F. Scott, then who are you?" He wanted her to know immediately that he was in on her joke. That they were on the same wavelength. Intellectual equals.

She held out her hand in formal greeting with a flourish. "Adeline's the name. Adeline Van Buren." It was the most beautiful name he had ever heard. It wasn't until later he discovered she'd stolen it from an American motorcycle adventurer.

They were both seventeen, both relatively tall, and both classified as 'gifted' by the county education authority. She was a viola prodigy, he excelled at mathematics. The five-day summer camp was an experiment of sorts: bring together a diverse range of young adults with different talents, set them a number of esoteric challenges, observe what happens and record the outcomes. Adeline felt that the whole thing may be a covert ploy by the government to unwittingly recruit the brightest minds of post-war Britain into a world of espionage and war game strategies. Scotty found this hard to believe. Professor Carmichael, the camp organiser, was a shambling figure with unkempt hair. Incredibly enthusiastic, but he seemed to be making things up as he went along.

Sitting beside each other that lunchtime, a chemical reaction took place between Scotty and Adeline. The initial teasing by Adeline (well received by Scotty), quickly fell into a more relaxed general discussion about the camp activities which, in turn, spiralled off tangentially into books, music, art, people. By the time the afternoon activities resumed, both were aware that something special had occurred. A new route had been established across a previously uncharted, mysteriously deep ocean. They both now had each other in common. A sincere interest in what the other was thinking. A joy shared when similarities of opinion were found. And laughter – so much laughter!

That afternoon, they were split into groups to work on different activities. Glances were stolen and secret smiles shared. Others began to notice, but said nothing. Scotty felt light-headed, overwhelmed by feeling this close to someone after such a short space of time. Adeline, more to the point, was a girl. A girl with long, straight auburn hair, held back in a simple band to reveal a swan neck. A girl with formidable intellect. A girl with a sense of the absurd and its potential for comedy. A girl with extraordinary skin. A girl with silver fire in her eyes.

At the end of the afternoon, the boys and girls were dispatched to their respective Nissen hut dormitories for 'reading and reflection' before dinner. Scotty didn't know what to do with himself. He lay on his bed and tried to read, but his mind was racing, his heart rate elevated. He stared blankly at the page before him, recollecting Adeline's words from lunchtime and testing out new, imaginary conversations in his head.

"What are you grinning at, old boy?" smirked Patrick Ross from the top bunk. "Has someone found love at the Carmichael Summer Camp for Gifted Idiots? That'll be a turn-up." Scotty smiled back at him, his non-denial speaking volumes.

In the dinner hall that evening, queueing with his tray at the serving counter, he spotted Adeline straight away. She was with a group of girls, sitting at a long table. She caught his eye and smiled. In an instant, he understood clearly that she wanted to sit beside him, but not without deserting her friends or inviting him to join the girls' table, which would be awkward. He smiled back and she understood clearly that they would have time to talk after dinner. What would Professor Carmichael make of this sudden outbreak of teenage telepathy?

After their rice pudding, Adeline and her friends got up from their table and, as she exited the dinner hall, she stopped by Scotty's table to discreetly say hello and pass on a small piece of paper, neatly folded into a square inch. He quickly slipped it into his back pocket and tried to look unflustered, failing miserably.

He raced back to the boys' hut and hurriedly locked himself in the lavatory, sitting down to unfold the note with the utmost care, like a lost piece of Egyptian papyrus. It was a poem by a modern writer Scotty was unaware of, handwritten in Adeline's delicate copperplate script. The poem was breathtakingly beautiful, saying nothing and everything simultaneously. Extraordinarily everyday and yet utterly unusual. It felt as if the poem had been written for them and them alone. Through

Adeline's actions, they had taken ownership of the words. Scotty read the poem over and over until there was a loud knock on the toilet door. He pulled the cistern chain and folded the note carefully into its square, placing it in the small inside pocket of his wallet. The note remained there, and in several other wallets, for many decades to come, its ink slowly fading and its edges gently fraying along the folds.

After dinner, the 'gifted youths' usually got together for a couple of hours' recreation in the camp café, formerly a NAAFI bar, that sold a slim variety of confectionery, chocolate and cordials as well as being home to a very old radiogram, an out-of-tune piano with several bare keys and a ping-pong table. Scotty and Adeline found themselves seated beside each other within a larger group of their cohorts, finding that this social environment suited their newfound friendship to a tee. They presented a united front to the others, politely finishing each other's sentences, reinforcing each other's jokes with infectious giggles and complementing each other's insights on a range of topics, both serious and frivolous. They felt elevated slightly from the crowd of blue stockings and bookworms surrounding them. They had discovered new colours that day. Hues that only they could discern. When Scotty returned from the bar counter with some soft drinks, Adeline placed her hand in his under the table and gently but significantly squeezed his palm as she continued to talk to a girl on the opposite side of the table. For the rest of the camp's duration, they were inseparable.

Ten minutes before lights out, they sneaked outside under the pretence of trying to locate Saturn in the night sky. Truly alone for the first time, they sat together on a low wall and looked up at the partially overcast sky, whispering to one another, skirting around the obvious whilst acknowledging everything by saying nothing. They looked down at their interlocked fingers, stealing glances into each other's eyes. They smiled, sweetly. They giggled. And then, the heavens opened and the air filled with a million heavy summer raindrops. Adeline stood up and whirled around in a circle, face upturned, laughing at the sky. Her friends emerged through the doors of the café to sweep her away to the safety of the girls' hut. Adeline briefly looked over her shoulder into Scotty's eyes. It was a mental snapshot that was to become indelibly etched into his soul. The door of the girls' hut slammed shut as they scampered inside, leaving Scotty standing in the rain, marvelling at the tremendous noise of the downpour enveloping him. He registered that his heart appeared to have expanded in size. There was a fullness in his chest that hadn't been there that morning.

*

Scotty and Patrick Ross were standing at the bar of the Drover's Inn, holding a pint of ale apiece. It was only 3pm, but this was their third drink of the day. The university term didn't start until Monday and they had some catching up to do, not having seen each other over the summer break. It was the usual routine of gradually getting pie-eyed while discussing their studies, their families, sport, current affairs, politics, music, books, girls and cars – not in any particular order and always with a high degree of silliness. Scotty was smoking Woodbines while Ross had taken to puffing on a pipe.

By the fourth pint, the pair had retired to a snug and it wasn't long before the conversation turned to Adeline. After the gifted youths camp all those years ago, Scotty and Adeline went their separate ways, promising to write to one another every week and telephone whenever opportunity allowed. Everything was just peachy for a while until Scotty's eighteenth birthday, when he was called up for National Service. Following his basic training, he was posted to Cyprus for eighteen months. It had been the best of times and the worst of times. A chance to see new bits of the world and make new friends. But also a feeling that something had been knocked out of him and that his innocence had been stripped away. He found it hard to write to Adeline any more. Something fundamental had changed inside of him. A hardening of his heart caused by too many NCOs barking in his face. And there were the two-day passes to Nicosia, where too much ouzo led invariably to regrettable liaisons involving affordable ladies with warm bodies and cold eyes. In the end, he simply allowed his correspondence with Adeline to peter out. He knew it would break her heart and, of course, it broke his too.

After his discharge from the army, he was accepted into a relatively reputable university studying applied mathematics. After three years on campus, he seemed to be settling into his new life and had found a routine of sorts. By chance, Patrick Ross was reading medicine at the college up the road, and the pair had decided to get digs together. At the beginning of the year's final term, on an impulse, he decided to write to Adeline for the first time in nearly five years. With a clear head, he woke one April morning just before sunrise and sat at his desk to compose a four-page epistle that he tried not to self-censor. He allowed his feelings to flow out onto the pages like spilled ink. Part humble apology, part biography, part hopeful invitation, he signed the letter (without a kiss) and placed it in a plain envelope. He took pride in remembering her postcode without having to look it up. Walking to the postbox at the end of the street, the stillness of the morning was exhilarating. The only sounds were his footsteps on the pavement, the dawn chorus, and the distant clink of milk bottles being delivered. He paused for a moment at the post box and then dropped the letter into the slot. Even if he never heard from Adeline again, he felt that this had been the right thing to do.

The following week, his heart flipped when he saw her neat handwriting lying on the porch doormat. He carried the letter with him to his morning tutorial, but didn't get a chance to read it until noon, when he was able to find a secluded corner of the library where he wouldn't be disturbed. She was pleased to hear from him. Delighted in fact. She understood why he hadn't written in so long. They were just kids and it wasn't as if they had been a proper couple after all. She had been busy too, growing up. Details of her current studies at a very reputable university about eighty miles away. Some remembrances of in-jokes and friends. A request to write again soon. A signature (with a kiss). Without overtly drawing attention to the fact, it was clear she was romantically unattached. He read the letter three or four times, and even held it up to the light in an attempt to decipher a couple of words that had been scored out and amended. Strolling across campus to the student canteen, he felt as if the air around him had become filled with extra oxygen. As if the atmospheric pressure had changed. He felt giddy and excited. For the first time in an age, he caught himself smiling as he listened to his inner thoughts, as he constructed imaginary dialogues between himself and Adeline once again.

With every letter, their feelings became more and more revelatory. Novels and records were exchanged, often with handwritten and heartfelt inscriptions. Expensive calls were made from public phone boxes on rainy nights. And, at the end of the summer term, plans were drawn up to meet in person. Scotty invested the last of his term-time allowance in a new sports jacket and a proper haircut. He caught the earliest train he could so they could spend the entire day together. She met him on the platform. Seeing her knocked him for six. The girl was now a young woman. Lovely in every way. Within minutes they had reverted to type. Her gentle teasing and unique take on life reducing him to tears of laughter. Her intellectual capacity was so much deeper than his. He hung on her every word, feeling like a dullard being guided out of his mundane world of numbers and equations into a sparkling universe of culture. Why she wanted to spend time with him, of all people, remained a mystery. But a mystery to be treasured.

And when it came for him to catch the last train home, they kissed on the station platform. A long, silent kiss in the darkness of the cool June air, with his fingers gently holding her neck. Afraid to break her.

July and August were a strange whirlwind. They settled into a routine of train journeys and day excursions. Polite introductions to parents were made. Little gifts were bought. And the letters continued to be written, this time with a more open sense of romance and always revealing some hidden emotion or new sweetness. And yes, love was mentioned. For it was as plain as day that this was love. First love, arrived late.

Physically, they indulged in lengthy 'necking' sessions whenever possible, but nothing more serious than that (for the moment). By the end of the summer, it was clear they were in a proper relationship. Boyfriend and girlfriend. Sweethearts. Two people with a deep affection for one another, who had taken some years to conquer the summit of their feelings, but were now still adjusting to the slightly overwhelming view and giddy atmosphere.

Adeline had returned to her university lodgings early in the week, but she had telephoned the previous night to tell Scotty she was miserable on campus and wanted to spend the weekend with him at his digs. After the phone call, Scotty found himself in a strange mood. They had never spent the night together and Adeline's request appeared to hint that they would be sleeping in the same bed. Although he was naturally excited about this new development, it caught him slightly off guard. It was unexpected, for a start. He had vaguely imagined an autumnal weekend away at a quiet seaside hotel, just the two of them, brandy in front of a log fire and all that nonsense. She was a sensitive girl and he wanted to do things right. He made a mental note to put clean sheets on his bed.

And now, here he was, sitting with Patrick in the snug, ordering his fifth pint of the afternoon.

"Dutch courage, old chap?" remarked Patrick with a sly grin. Scotty had to admit he was feeling a little tiddly. Just a little.

Leaving the pub half an hour later, he half-walked, half-jogged through the cobbled streets towards the station. He was running late and realised he must look a bit of a state. After the darkness of the pub, the autumn sunset seemed unusually bright. When he finally arrived at the station, he saw Adeline waiting at the entrance, holding a small overnight case with both hands. She looked a little smaller than normal somehow. Upon seeing him her face lit up and then almost instantly dimmed, just a fraction, as she realised he'd been drinking. Apologising profusely for his tardiness, he grabbed her bag and said he'd like to treat her to a hearty dinner at The Drover's to cheer her up. On the way back to the pub, she chatted a little about how miserable she had been over the last few days. And, although Scotty nodded in agreement and said all the right, comforting things, he couldn't help feeling that she'd rained on his parade a little. He'd been having a tremendously carefree Saturday in the pub with Patrick and now things seemed very earnest and serious.

Back at the pub, a crowd of fellow students had joined Patrick. Mostly male, with a few females. Adeline was introduced to 'the gang' and sat down between Scotty and a girl everyone called Jude (despite the fact her real name was Emily) who was an opinionated sort with a rather severe French bob. Pints of beer and glasses of wine were ordered, plates of food arrived, cigarettes and pipes were smoked, jokes were cracked and laughed at. Scotty found himself caught up in a conversation at one end of the table about politics – one of those terrible instances where the talk seemed to simply go around in circles and no one could really tell if they were in agreement or at loggerheads. Adeline chatted mostly with the girl called Jude, but he could tell they didn't have a lot in common from the way she held herself, arms loosely crossed over her chest. Jude appeared to be doing most of the talking – bragging about her travels by the sound of it. By 9pm, Scotty's eyelids were beginning to droop and his speech was slurring. With a little coaxing, Adeline managed to shepherd him out of the pub as he looked over his shoulder making his fond farewells and saluting towards Ross. Once outside, he had to immediately go back in to get his matches. Through the window, Adeline could see him rapidly finishing off a dram of whisky that Patrick had hastily put in front of him.

Fifteen minutes later, Scotty was fumbling with his keys trying to open the door to his flat. Walking home arm in arm, he'd sung a rather bawdy song he had learned in the army, much to the amusement of Adeline who appeared to have relaxed a little now that they were away from the clamour of the pub. They made their way to his bedroom at the back of the house.

"Bugger," he mumbled as he realised he hadn't changed the bed sheets. "Back in a tick." He stumbled off to use the outside lav, returning some time later with new bedsheets and two cups of milky tea. After helping him to make up the bed, Adeline took a seat rather awkwardly at his writing desk, drinking her tea.

In the quietness, Scotty tried to stifle a belch. Finishing his tea, he got up and proceeded to unbuckle the belt of his trousers. Startled, Adeline quickly said, "Is it okay if I have the room to myself for a bit?" With a sudden realisation, Scotty understood that she probably wasn't keen on undressing in front of him. He wasn't in Nicosia now. "Of course! Of course, old girl. I'll absent myself for a bit." He waited outside the room and smoked a Woodbine. Eventually, she appeared in the hallway in a nightdress and disappeared quickly into the tiny bathroom to brush her teeth. Meanwhile he returned to bed, stripping down to his shorts. Presently, she scuttled through the doorway and quickly switched off the little lamp on his desk, plunging the room into darkness. She crept in under the covers and he held her in his arms.

After some whispered chat about their evening and some further apologies for being 'a bit tipsy', Scotty began kissing Adeline, gently at first and then with a greater sense of urgency and passion. Despite his intake of alcohol, he was a young red-blooded man and, before long, a rather obvious physiological transformation began to occur. He pulled Adeline closer to him and kissed her harder, tracing his hand down the contour of her hips and thighs to find the edge of her nightdress. Just as he was about to pull the hem northwards, her body tensed and she sat up in bed with an emphatic, "No, James." It was the first time she had ever referred to him as anything other than Scotty. He came back down to earth with a bump, feeling like a chastised child. A wave of muddy guilt passed through his body as his muscles relaxed. He sank back within himself.

"Look, it's just that…" she began to say.

"It's okay, darling. Quite okay. Entirely my fault," he said.

She lay down once again and turned onto her side, facing away from him. Finally, the booze took its toll and he found he could fight unconsciousness no longer. As he dissolved into oblivion, he heard Adeline give a quiet, sad sigh.

The next morning Scotty woke late to find a note on his desk. "Had to dash for the train. Will call you at 7pm." No kiss.

Bugger. The pulsating headache behind his eyes rapidly peaked in its intensity, leaving him no option but to fall back onto the bed and into an uneasy slumber for the rest of the morning and most of the afternoon.

Two days later, Scotty picked up Adeline from the station in Patrick's little car (a sporty green roadster purchased for 'a song' from a chum of Patrick's called 'Silver Jimmy'). They had arranged to have one final day-trip before she returned to university. On the phone the previous night she had been distant, blaming tiredness for her unusual mood. It was a drizzly day with an unpleasantly chilly breeze. They set off with no particular plan and simply travelled from village to village, eventually arriving at a piece of woodland with a Victorian folly.

Something had changed between them, quite drastically. Gone was the teasing and laughter and intellectual insights, replaced with silence and stiff conversation about nothing in particular. Scotty tried to recapture the lighthearted sweetness of previous times, but it was no good. Adeline was expecting to hear something quite specific from Scotty's lips, and he was well aware of this, but words failed him. More worryingly, he wasn't quite sure if words needed to be said at all. Somehow, he felt hurt, despite accepting full responsibility for their current state of affairs. They climbed to the top of the folly to admire the view of the surrounding countryside. It was rather bleak and uninspiring. Scotty put his arm around Adeline's shoulders but, although she didn't make a big deal of things, he could tell it was an unwelcome advance. They returned to the car and drove back the way they had come in silence. He offered to drive her home to her parents' house, but she insisted on taking the train. He parked up outside the station, hoping to have time to resolve matters but, as soon as he pulled on the handbrake, she hopped out of the passenger door and said, "I really have to go now. Goodbye Scotty." And, with that, she disappeared into the station without looking back once.

Scotty sat in the car for a very long time, thinking things over. Whether from a sense of male pride, stubbornness or sheer stupidity, he failed to get out of the car and go after her. Eventually, he set off for the Drover's Inn, where he had arranged to meet Patrick for a quick pint and return the car keys.

Over the following weeks, he wrote three letters to Adeline, each one shorter than its predecessor. He didn't receive any letters in return. In the end, he decided to give up trying to contact her and resolved that the whole sorry affair was best forgotten. Live and learn. Time to move on. By December, he was courting a pretty nurse called Elsa that Patrick had introduced him to.

*

Scotty's knees felt stiff. He knew he'd have to be careful standing up later on. He'd been in the attic for thirty minutes, searching for an old pension policy document. As usual, he'd become sidetracked looking through the boxes of goodness-knows-what lurking up here in the dark. Ice skates. Italian tourist maps. Scrapbooks with birthday cards, stamps, pressed flowers and newspaper cuttings. Tucked away in a corner, he found a shoebox with an elastic band wrapped around its middle. Inside, a stack of old letters from Adeline, and others, but mostly Adeline. There were some photos too. A group photo of the gifted youths and one of Scotty and Adeline standing in front of a Nissen hut. Looking at the image filled him with a viscous sensation. Regret? Nostalgia? His heart felt heavy in his chest, despite the involuntary smile that had appeared on his face.

The young man in the photo looked out at the older, crumbling version of himself. Bespectacled. Frayed at the edges. Hair receding and considerably greyer. The youthful jawline transformed into middle-aged jowls.

Over the years, he'd often wondered about Adeline. They'd only really spent a handful of days in each other's company – and yet his mind would wander back to her more often than any of the other old flames from his single days. (What was the name of that nurse again? Eloise?)

He had spotted Adeline in the newspapers a few times over the years and heard her on the radio once. She was Doctor Adeline now and an authority on modern educational methods. Fiercely intellectual, vocally principled and quite tough by all accounts. She was a government adviser which, even in these enlightened times, must still have its challenges for a woman. Once, on a visit to the local lending library with the children, he stumbled across a publication of hers in the non-fiction section. The author's photo on the inside of the dust jacket revealed that she, too, was grey now. The crow's feet around her eyes hinted that she'd enjoyed plenty of laughter over the years and, even though she was striking a serious pose for the camera, her mouth was still just a few degrees away from a smirk. The blurb revealed that she lived in Somerset with her husband and had two children. He reflected on the fact that he lived in Finchley with his wife and also had two children, the eldest about to head off to university. Despite the fact he didn't have a PhD or any publications to his name, he liked to think of himself as a relatively happy soul. Financial director for a firm that made camping equipment. Petrol mower in the garden shed. Shiny Rover in the driveway. New television set in the living room. Dinner parties with erudite friends (including Dr Patrick Ross, the esteemed psychiatrist). Holidays in Spain. Golf club membership. He was happy with his lot.

But looking at the faded photo of himself and Adeline, it was only natural to think about what his life, and hers, might have been like if things had gone differently. They were certainly deeply in love all those years ago. And then there was the army. And then university. And then that rekindling of the romance that had burned in such a haphazard way across the course of one fateful summer. His boorish behaviour. Her distance on that final day. And then her silence. Confirming, in his mind at least, that they had both realised they weren't really suited to one another after all. He was convinced that, in any alternate universe, they would always end up at the same place. Separate entities with a briefly shared history.

At times like these, he fleetingly considered writing to her care of her publisher's office. A short note to simply reaffirm the fact that, once upon a time, they had shared something special. Something that had been replaced with a dim and distant feeling that rose to the surface every so often, when he heard a particular piece of music or picked up a certain book. A note to simply wish her well. That was all, and that was enough. But he knew that the letter would never be written and that was, more than likely, for the best.

He placed the elastic band around the shoebox and switched off the bare bulb in the attic, climbing down the swing ladder with one knee audibly clicking, his bifocals perched precariously on the end of his nose. The pension document stated that he could retire in five years and look forward to a relatively comfortable dotage. As he pushed the ladder back up into the attic he wondered where the hell the years had gone. Really, where had they gone?

On the last evening of the camp, there was a special dinner with cake and an awards ceremony. Adeline won a prize for being first to solve a particularly tricky logic problem and Scotty felt a curious sense of pride when she collected her book token to a hearty round of applause from the group. After the dinner dishes had been collected and washed, everyone made their way to the camp café as usual but, grabbing Scotty by the hand, Adeline suggested they sneak off to watch the sun go down from 'the hill' – a little mound at the edge of the camp with a single tree at its summit.

Scotty sat with his back to the trunk, allowing Adeline to rest her back against his chest. They had never been so close. The fragrance of her hair was intoxicating. He could feel the rise and fall of her chest as she breathed. As they chatted quietly, they faced the same direction, towards the horizon where the sun had emerged below a low bank of pink clouds, making its eternal descent.

"I wish we didn't have to go home tomorrow," he said. It was a silly, childish statement to make, but it genuinely reflected how he felt.

"And to think, last week I didn't really want to come to this silly camp!" she laughed.

There was a pause. Their first comfortable silence.

"If we go our separate ways tomorrow and we don't stay in touch, we don't see one another ever again, what will become of us?" she asked.

"But of course we'll stay in touch!" he said, with just a hint of anxiety in his voice. He wasn't quite sure where the conversation was heading.

"I know we will, silly, but let's imagine that we don't. Let's say that this is the last time we will ever see one another. What will happen to us?"

"You mean the 'us' from right here, in this moment, sitting under this tree watching the sun go down?" he asked.

After a moment, she said, "We'll turn into ghosts."

Neither of them said anything for a while. A breeze caught

a strand of her hair and played with it.

"We'll just be memories in other people's minds. The people we become in the future. They'll be different people from us. Literally composed of different atoms to us. So we – the Scotty and Adeline of this very moment – will become ghosts. Ghosts that haunt our future selves."

She smiled a wistful smile, but there was a sadness to her words.

At first he struggled to follow her train of thought, but gradually the notion became clear in his mind. He found himself enjoying the thought experiment.

"They say that highly emotional events create more indelible memories," he said. "So, if we are to become ghosts, we may stick around here for decades to come."

She nestled back into his chest a little as he continued to talk.

"Think about what a ghost is: a part of a human soul that can't move forward in time, due to some unfinished earthly business, haunting a specific place or person for years, unaware of the spectral nature of their own ghostliness and unaware of the havoc they may be causing. If you think about the basic definition, I think we may fit the bill, Adeline old girl."

She continued to look towards the setting sun and said, "I'm not sure if I like the idea of being a ghost, trapped forever in a moment."

He took her hand. "I think that all depends on the moment in question. And besides, I quite like the thought of being haunted by you."

She turned a little to look into his eyes, the last few rays of sunlight sparkling in her own, not quite smiling. Tomorrow, they would have to say their fond farewells. But, for now, they had this moment. They would always have this moment.

About the author

W. Terence Walsh (b. 1929) is the fictional author of the stories contained within this collection. An only child, he was educated at a minor public school in England, served for a brief time in the army under the National Service Act, and then spent most of his working life in the civil service, working as a researcher and behavioural scientist. A bachelor with no children, he lived a relatively solitary existence. He did, however, have a close circle of correspondents who were fascinated with ghost stories, the supernatural and fiction in general – especially the short story format. In May 1978, he failed to appear at his office desk one Monday morning (he had never before had a day of absence in his working life). When the police were called to his home in the picturesque village of Summerhill in Kent, they found everything in immaculate condition. All the household bills had been paid in full and his bank account had been emptied a few days earlier. A buff envelope had been laid carefully on the dining table, with an Indian elephant's claw bell positioned neatly on top alongside a set of house keys. The manuscript that was found inside the envelope has been published in this book, in its entirely, including this footnote. W. Terence Walsh was never seen or heard of again.

Sincere thanks

Some truly remarkable people helped in the production of this book. In no particular order, sincere thanks go to Kris Johnston, Roger Kerr, Sam Healy (who have introduced the author to so much great literature over many years, and have provided invaluable feedback on this manuscript), David McCurry, Jonathan McHugh, Peter McAdam (who co-created the idea behind *The Burden*), David Jack, Chris Howard, Kelly Pierce, Heather Hughes, May Hughes, Steve Todd, Rob Connell, Richard Happer, Iain Sangster, Tony Bibby, Malcolm Thompson, Tony Jordan, Tara West, Sarah Robinson, Robert F Mack, Dr Ben Fletcher-Watson (whose input on structure and tone was incredibly useful), my brother Glenn and, of course, my amazing wife and children.

Printed in Great Britain
by Amazon

51354372R00102